CANAPÉ-VERT

PRIZE WINNING NOVEL

Second Latin American Contest

Woodcut by Edward Larocque Tinker

CANAPÉ-VERT

by PHILIPPE THOBY-MARCELIN
and PIERRE MARCELIN

translated by EDWARD LAROCQUE TINKER

FARRAR & RINEHART INC.

New York   Toronto

This book was designed and decorated by
EDWARD LAROCQUE TINKER

CAST

HUMAN, SUPERHUMAN, AND ANIMAL

A

ACTÉON: Son of Dorvilus.

AGAMAN: Famous chameleon loa.

AGASU: See General Anglessou.

ALADIN: A small farmer, about thirty years old. Sanite was his mistress but he was in love with Florina.

ALTIDOR: Ti-Dan's dead father.

ANACIUS: Child of Zinzin and Carmen and brother of Orphise.

ANILUS: A rheumatic friend of Norvil.

ASSEZLHOMME: Farmer of Carrefour-Laboule.

B

BACOULOU: A famous fighting cock belonging to Zinzin.

BÊBÊ: The deaf-mute servant of Sor Tia.

BOBO: An inhabitant of Canapé-Vert.

BONACCUEIL: Zinzin's country cousin from Carrefour-Laboule and the owner of a good fighting cock called Gros-Sirop.

BOISPIRHAUT: A famous houngan, or Vodun priest.

BOSSA: See Tonton Bossa.

BOUQUI: The goat in the folk tales who always made a fool of himself.

C

CARMEN: Zinzin's wife and the mother of Anacius and Orphise.

CICIE: See Madan Bossa.

CHOLO: A peasant of Carrefour-Laboule.

CIUS: The son of Sor Na, and an uncommonly clever thief.

D

DAMBALLA OUEDDO: The chief Rada deity, also called the "Master of Heaven."

DÉMOISSIÉ: The host at a Danse Congo.

DESVALLONS: A well-to-do landowner.

DIEUJUSTE: A peasant of Carrefour-Laboule.

DIVESCO: The owner of the cockpit.

DORISMÉ: A guest at Démoissié's party.

DORVILUS: Also called Judge Dor, was chef de section, a sort of county official who combined the duties of justice of the peace with those of sheriff.

E

ELIVOIS: A peasant of Carrefour-Laboule.

ERZILIE FRÉDA DAHOMEY: See Grande Erzilie.

EXANTHUS: A son of Tonton Bossa by his second wife, Madan Bossa (Sor Cicie).

F

FLORIAN: One of Sarah's neighbors, who acts as a stooge for the houngan Préval.

FLORINA: The daughter of Prévilon and Lamercie, and granddaughter of Grande Da, a pretty girl of sixteen for whose sake Aladin deserted Sanite.

FRÉQUENT: Dorvilus' dog.

G

GENERAL ANGLESSOU: Known as the "Bucket of Blood," a fierce Petro god, who "mounts" Aladin and forces him to commit a horrible crime.

GRANDE DA: The mother of Prévilon and the grandmother of Florina. She is a mambo, or Vodun priestess.

GRANDE ERZILIE: The African Venus, or goddess of love and font of creation, who "possesses" Grande Da and speaks through her mouth.

GRAND-ORIENT: Dorvilus' cook, stolen by Cius.

GROS-MOCEAU: Desvallons' tenant farmer.

GROS-SIROP: Bonaccueil's fighting cock.

GUÉDÉ: Is used as a general designation for spirits or loas and also as the specific name of a particular African god. (See Papa Gedenibo.)

J

JEANLUSSE: An inseparable friend of Kinda.

JOSAPHAT: Son of Tonton Bossa by his first wife, Ti-Tante. He changed his name to José when he was in Cuba.

JOSÉ: See Josaphat.

JUDGE DOR: See Dorvilus.

K

KINDA: An inseparable friend of Jeanlusse.

L

LAMERCIE: Wife of Prévilon and mother of Florina.

LEGBA: See Papa Legba.

LOUISINA: Farmer of Carrefour-Laboule.

M

MADAN BOSSA: The second wife of Tonton Bossa and the mother of Vital, Exanthus, and Philoxène. She is a younger sister of Grande Da and Florina's aunt. Madan is Creole for Madame. She is frequently called Sor Cicie.

MALICE: A shrewd folklore character who always gets the better of Bouqui.

MÉLIE: See Sor Mélie.

MÉZINE: The favorite mistress of Dorvilus.

N

NA: See Sor Na.

NIBO: See papa Gedenibo.

NORMIL: Owner of a bar and gambling joint frequented by Prévilon.

O

OGOUN BADAGRIS: A Rada loa or deity.

ORPHISE: The daughter of Zinzin and Carmen.

P

PAPA LEGBA: Alias Baron Carrefour, is a Rada spirit or loa, who acts as prime minister for Damballa Oueddo. Every appeal to the latter must be preceded by a service and sacrifice to Papa Legba.

PHILOXÈNE: Son of Tonton Bossa and his second wife.

PRÉVAL: A well-known young houngan, whom Sarah asks to help Sanite regain her lover.

PRÉVILON: The son of Grande Da, the husband of Lamercie, and the father of Florina.

PAPA GEDENIBO: Also called Guédé and Nibo, is the plebeian god beloved by the very black people and disdained by the mulattoes. He is almost the only important loa that originated in Haiti. Control of the region of the dead is vested in him, and he serves as prime minister for the chief Petro god, Baron Samedi, just as Papa Legba does for Damballa Oueddo.

R

ROYE: Is a Creole contraction of Roi Loangue. He was an ancient African king, now believed to be a powerful loa.

S

SANITE: The washerwoman mistress of Aladin, whom he casts off.

SARAH: A town prostitute who harbors her cousin Sanite.

SOR: Means "sister" in Creole.

SOR CICIE: See Madan Bossa.

SOR MÉLIE: The keeper of a general store and bar at the crossroads, where everyone in Canapé-Vert and the neighboring hamlets congregated to gossip.

SOR NA: The mother of the wastrel, Cius.

Sor Tia: The principal wife of Dorvilus, with whom he lived officially.

Sor Ti-Ma: Jeanlusse's wife.

T

Ti: Means simply "little."

Tia: See Sor Tia.

Ti-Dan: A peasant of Canapé-Vert who took Dorvilus' position as chef de section.

Ti-Ma: See Sor Ti-Ma.

Ti-Macelin: The town dog-catcher.

Ti-Mouché: Dorvilus' assistant.

Tiodor: A judge, or chef de section, who oppressed the people.

Ti-Tante: Tonton Bossa's first wife, who died of a broken heart because he discarded her for Cicie. She was the mother of José.

Tonton Bossa: A clever houngan whose failure to keep his pact with Baron Samedi brought down a curse on the Valley and all its inhabitants. His first wife was Ti-Tante, by whom he had José, and his second was Sor Cicie, who blessed him with three sons, Vital, Exanthus, and Philoxène, all three of whom became zombis.

Ti-Rouge: He took Ti-Mouché's place as assistant to Dorvilus.

Tonton: Means "uncle."

V

Vilbon: A farmer of Carrefour-Laboule.

Vital: Son of Tonton Bossa and his second wife.

Z

Zinzin: An inhabitant of Canapé-Vert who owned a famous fighting cock, called Bacoulou.

HAITIAN BACKGROUND

HAITI is a brave, persistent little republic with a tragic, blood-drenched past. Columbus set foot on her shores on his initial voyage and she became the earliest center of Spanish colonization. Her first inhabitants, the Caribs, were soon well on the way to extermination under the implacable whips of the gold-hungry conquistadores; and, to save the few survivors, the benign Padre Las Casas suggested to the Spanish crown that they be replaced by Negro slaves, who had far stronger constitutions.

A few blacks were imported in the first decade of the sixteenth century, but it was not until Las Casas' suggestion was acted upon that they were sent over in large numbers and the slave trade became a thriving business. The white colonists, however, in their greed for chattel manpower, were not content to buy only docile Negroes from the Gold Coast, like the gentle adaptable Congos, but began to purchase members of the fierce warrior tribes of the interior of Africa—Agonas, Socos, Fantins, Judas, Aradas, Bissagots, and Sosos. This was one of the primary causes of the bloody disaster that eventually overwhelmed them, for among these slaves were chiefs and sor-

cerers, who kept alive the spirit of independence
through the catalyzing influence of the Vodun cult.
It was an independence that, in spite of the repres-
sions of a cruel bondage, manifested itself in revolt
after revolt, beginning in 1533, that continued until,
in defiance of France, England, and Spain, the foundation of the first Black Republic on the American
continent emerged from a sea of blood in 1804.

But the habit of rebellion was strong and, even
after the whites had been driven out, sanguinary con-
flicts took place between rival leaders and between
the blacks and mulattoes. Even a few evanescent in-
tervals of empire occurred. In these upheavals all the
great sugar mills were destroyed and the land that
slave labor had made the particular gem of Les Isles
sous les Vents, a veritable Golconda for its European
masters, fell into a state of primitive agriculture and
economic and political disorder.

However, the unquenchable addiction to liberty
survived bloodshed, poverty, and all attempts at
domination, both foreign and domestic, and at every
opportunity Haiti did all in her power to help others
to gain that freedom she cherished so passionately.
Few know that a contingent of Haitians fought side
by side with our Continental soldiers in the American
Revolution. It happened in this way: When France
was our ally, Admiral Count d'Estaing recruited 800
men of color, who composed a regiment of chasseurs,
and sailed from the island to Savannah, Georgia,

where our troops were heavily beset by the English. They landed on the American coast in 1779 and, with other French reinforcements, joined in an attack on the British line. They must have been a brave sight in their brilliant blue coats with green lapels and small white buttons, their breeches of white cloth with white gaiters, and their headgear ornamented with yellow and white plumes. This attack was followed by a dashing bayonet charge on an English column; the enemy was driven back into his fort, whose artillery opened up on the chasseurs, killing or wounding many of them.

The Count d'Estaing later returned to the island and recruited another expedition, this time aimed at Florida, and 303 Haitian men of color fought under him at the Battle of Pensacola.

The Black Republic also aided South America in her fight for freedom. When Francisco Miranda took refuge on the island, its emperor Dessalines presented him with a handsome Haitian banner: tearing off the yellow portion of a Spanish flag, Miranda· sewed it on the other, and flew this at his masthead as he sailed away on his next attempt to free Venezuela. When that country finally attained independence it was this flag that she adopted as her national standard.

Bolivar, remembering this when he was a refugee in Kingston, Jamaica, and had been refused assistance by the major powers, turned to Haiti for help. In 1816, President Pétion supplied him with men, money, and munitions, exacting in return only a promise that when Venezuela had been liberated the slaves would be set free.

No land knew better the evils of slavery than Haiti, and it was natural that she take the lead in its abolition. Her serfs were freed in 1804, three decades before England declared human bondage illegal, and more than half a century before Lincoln signed the Emancipation Proclamation.

Haiti's unconquerable spirit has been justified, for today our sister republic of the Antilles, who has again declared with the forces of freedom, is enjoying her greatest era of progress and prosperity.

In spite of her harried past, she has been able to produce a group of men of learning, doctors, scientists and writers, many of whom were educated in the best universities and medical schools of France —a poet like their beloved Oswald Durand, an ethnographer and author like Dr. Price-Mars, a philologist and folklorist like Mr. Jules Faine, to list but a few. But this highly literate part of the population, according to Dr. Price-Mars, amounts to only between ten and fifteen per cent, who rule the country, fill all the offices of government, both civil and military, and manage the businesses of any importance. The balance, some four-fifths of the people, are largely illiterate peasant laborers and small farmers.

This majority practices the religion bequeathed them by their African ancestors, for the *houngans,* or Vodun priests, brought to Haiti in the reeking holds of slave ships, established in the new land a priestly hierarchy, whose knowledge and theology have been transmitted in an unbroken line.

Their pantheon, roughly speaking, is composed of innumerable gods, *loas, mystères,* and spirits—all different names for the same thing—who are divided into two main groups, or "families" as they are called. One, the Arada or Rada, has only beneficent gods, who never work evil. Their original habitat was Dahomey and their chief deity Damballa Oueddo, the Master of Heaven. It is to him that a man prays and makes offering to secure favors for himself and his family. He can only be approached, however, through the intervention of Papa Legba, old and lame, the guardian of the gate; so any appeal to Damballa must be preceded by a service and sacrifice to Papa Legba.

The principal female deity is Grande Erzilie or Erzilie Fréda, who must not be confused with the red-eyed Erzilie ge-rouge who belongs to the Petro clan and works evil. Grande Erzilie works only good, and is the black Venus, or goddess of love, the embodiment of all female charms. She has no children and has taken all the men of Haiti as her collective spouse. Thursdays and Saturdays are hers, and on those days innumerable candles are lighted in her honor. A very jealous goddess, she devotes herself to furthering the interests of her male worshipers and defeating the matrimonial schemes of all young women. Only widows and very old females who have given up all hope of the pleasures of the flesh ever dare to petition her aid.

The other family of gods is the Petro, originally from the Congo. They work evil, so it is to them that prayers are addressed to secure the illness or death of an enemy; and, as they always exact an horrific payment for favors granted, they are much feared. Their chief loa is Baron Samedi, Lord of the Cemetery, and it is his malign influence that permeates this entire novel and causes all the misfortunes that transform it into a black version of a Greek tragedy.

Gede or Guédé (sometimes called Papa Gedenibo) belongs to both groups and is probably the only important loa that originated in Haiti. He has a bawdy, Bacchic flavor, loves rum laced with hot pepper and a touch of nutmeg, and his devotees placate him with the foods he likes greedily—parched corn and peanuts placed on a white plate at the foot of his cross. Gay, rowdy, and a scandalous jester, he always dresses in rusty top hat, long black coat, and ragged trousers, and has a cigar sticking out of the corner of his mouth. Beloved by the blacks, he is scorned by the mulattoes, because he is essentially the plebeian god.

He controls the regions of the dead, dictates everything that happens there, and renders more or less the same services to Baron Samedi that Papa Legba does to Damballa Oueddo. Always invisible, he manifests himself—as do all the other gods and loas—by "possessing" one of his human worshipers and speaking through his mouth. It is called "mounting" in the Creole dialect and the person so "mounted" is known as a "horse." Whenever anyone in this condition begins to speak with the voice of Guédé, his first words are invariably "Parlay cheval ou" (Tell my horse) and this may be the origin of our slang phrase "Straight from the horse's mouth!" What makes Guédé so particularly popular with the *ti-nègres*, or poor blacks, is that, whenever he "possesses" them, he takes the opportunity of poking satirical fun at their betters and employers: which arouses reasonable suspicion that, in some instances at least, his worshipers feign a "mounting" so that they can safely unburden their minds.

The catalogue of Vodun divinities is long-drawn-out, so only two more will be mentioned in order to complete the list of those who take part in the action of this book—General Anglessou (sometimes Agasu), one of the Rada cycle, and Roye, an ancient Congo king, known as Roi Loangue, who became a powerful loa.

Almost every household has a *houmfor,* or Vodun temple, consisting of a small room housing a shrine dedicated to the particular loa that watches over its welfare, and a *tonnelle*, or palm-thatched shed without sides, in whose shade the various Vodun rites and dances take place. No act is performed without due consideration of the probable reaction of the nether world, and these black people are so enmeshed in a tangle of taboos, that they appear to be living in a land of spirits, ruled by loas and mystères, whom they must woo and obey to gain their ends and to avoid death and disaster. Indeed these ancestral credences are so inextricably entangled in the very brain fiber of the people that they exert visible physical effects, and the man, or woman, who thinks he has offended a loa, or has been bewitched by houngan or *ouanga* charm, will sicken and die by the force of his belief in the efficacy of magic.

There is, too, a stubborn conviction that when a Vodun priest dies, or one thought to possess great *connaisance*, or influence with the mystères, his soul becomes a powerful loa that will do great harm to its relatives, unless it be removed from the body by a houngan and confined for a certain time in an earthen crock. This is the explanation of the scene where Boispirhaut performs the elaborate ceremony of removing Tonton Bossa's loa at his funeral.

The adaptability of the Negro race, which permitted it to live in Haiti under conditions which destroyed the Carib, and which has always been a guaranty of its survival, made it possible for the Negroes to accept the tenets of the Catholic Church taught them by their erstwhile owners without in any way abandoning their ancestral belief in Vodon cult. While there has been a certain integration between the two, it is only a surface one, and they are practiced concurrently. The result is a most bizarre mélange, for the pagan ceremonies are always preceded by the singing of Catholic litanies and the recitation of prayers of the Virgin, this part of the ceremony being generally conducted by a *prêtre savane* or "bush priest," as the colored sacristans of Catholic chapels are called.

The fact that pictures of the saints are often found on the Vodun altars has encouraged the thought that there is a closer relationship between the two beliefs than exists in reality. The truth is quite simple. No Haitian artist has ever depicted loa or mystère except in cabalistic geometrical figures called *Vêvès*, drawn on the ground with flour, and these simple black people hungered for a more lifelike representation of their guardian spirits. Knowing that the serpent was sacred to Damballa, when they saw a picture of St. Patrick and his snakes in the booths devoted to religious objects, they bought it and placed it on the altar in their houmfors as a representation of their god. In the same way, when they were taught that the Virgin Mary was the acme of spirituality and beauty of life, they chose her portrait, with no thought of irreverence, to personify their pagan Venus, Grande Erzilie, who was to them the essence of all feminine desirability and the font of created life.

The very people who danced through Saturday night to the beat of tom-toms in Vodun ceremonies, will attend mass the next morning as devout and decorous Catholics. To them there is no inconsistency in practicing the two faiths simultaneously, for they feel no conflict between them. Both teach a belief in a Supreme Being and the immortality of the soul and, in their minds, their loas and mystères are the equivalent of the Catholic saints and angels. This makes a bridge to understanding, and they think that, if they are assiduous in both, they will thereby double their chances of success in this world and salvation in the next. It is a little like the "shotgun" remedies of the old-fashioned country doctors.

The zombi remains one of the unsolved mysteries of Haiti. The belief in their existence is omnipresent among the peasantry, who are firmly convinced that certain *bocors* and houngans have the power of producing a trance condition, closely resembling death, in any person they choose and that after the victim's burial, the sorcerers visit the grave, disinter the "corpse," and administer an antidote that brings it back to partial life. These semiresurrected bodies are called zombis and have no memory of their identity or past. They never speak, are quite unconscious of their surroundings, and walk as if in a trance. However, they will obey commands and can be made to work tirelessly and without recompense.

In this fact lies the motive, because the bocors can make the zombis slave for their personal profit or can sell them to planters in distant parts of the country where the poor souls will not be recognized. Their owners, however, must be careful to prevent the zombis from getting a single grain of salt in their food, for if they do, it is believed that their memories return and they will run back to their graves, dig in, and die—this time beyond any hope of resuscitation.

The ignorant are so sure that houngans have this power that they take every precaution to secure their relatives from a zombi fate by stabbing the corpse, or removing the heart, before burial.

Many insist that zombis are merely a figment of the superstitious African mind: but zombis have been photographed and various writers, who have seen them, report that they are not just village idiots and that they live in a tragic, dissociated aura that precludes any such simple theory.

There have been several tentative explanations of this weird condition. Hypnotism is the most usual and gains a certain credence from the belief that the houngans are familiar with its use and, if the tales of certain travel-writers are correct, they even have the power of hypnotizing snakes so that they will be straight and rigid like a walking stick.

Secret drugs, known to the bocors, also have been suggested, drugs that paralyze those areas of the human brain that control speech, memory, and will power. New corroboration of this theory is to be found in a book called *The Empire of the Snakes*, published by Stokes in 1935. Its author, F. G. Carnochan, went to Africa, where he gained the confidence of the natives and was initiated into the secret Snake Society. He learned the primitive method of immunization against snakebite used by the Africans for some centuries before the white man discovered his scientific, but no more effective, technique. But what is of more interest here, he became acquainted with the properties of a certain mysterious drug called "kingo" or "kingolio." Taken to a rocky plateau, known only to the priests of the Serpent Cult, he was shown this strange bushlike plant. It had long narrow leaves, of a deep glossy green like the mountain laurel. Dozens of inch-thick stems shot up from a common root, with tips ending in lashlike tendrils that dipped toward the earth and bored into the soil. This was probably the way in which it reproduced itself, for it showed no evidence of flower or seed. The root was bright orange-red, and from the main stem innumerable long slim fibers extended in every direction and took hold in the crevices of the rocks. "It was the bark of these cable-like roots that produced a powder that turned men into marionettes." It robbed the taker of all will power and transformed him into a robot that moved only when it was directed.

The author, who brought back samples of this root which he presented to a medical college for experimentation, describes how the chief sorcerer gave some of it to a young Negro, who immediately appeared to lose all individual will. He was ordered to place his tongue on a heavy wooden stool and a stout thorn was driven through it. Then on command, he stood up with the stool hanging from his tongue and displayed no sense of pain whatsoever.

Carnochan himself later took a small dose of this plant and found that, although he did not lose consciousness, it paralyzed certain areas of his brain, particularly the part that governs the motor nerves, for he could not move, and all will, energy, and initiative were dead.

This is a physical condition paralleling that of the zombi and raises the interesting question as to whether the Vodun priests, who were brought from

Africa to Haiti as slaves, did not find the kingolio growing wild on the island, or bring with them cuttings or seeds of the plant (if there were any).

These theories are merely tentative and the true explanation awaits verification by some trained scientist who will make a careful study on the ground.

While the small literate governing class speaks Standard French, the balance of the population use the Creole Dialect. Soft, suave, and saturated with exotic lure, it is a sister to the patois of Martinique and the "gombo" of the Negroes of Louisiana. Sometimes a word or two sounds like French and then, to the uninitiated, it trails off into a jumble of meaningless, but musical syllables, as smooth and rounded as warm butter. It was a daughter of necessity, for, when the slavers loaded their ships on the Gold Coast with human merchandise for Haiti, they were careful to choose Negroes from different tribes who could not understand each other's speech. It was a precaution against concerted uprising and the same plan was followed by Creole planters in recruiting their *ateliers,* or slave gangs. As a result the *bossals,* as African-born serfs were called, found themselves in a strange land unable to understand the language of their masters or even to communicate with many of their fellows in misfortune, who spoke different tribal tongues.

French, which had taken centuries to develop into its present subtle, intricate form, was far too complex for these simple Africans. So they did their best and contrived a queer, simplified "pigeon" dialect of their own. It would be impossible to describe the myriad ways in which the tongues of African slaves mutilated and amputated the French language. But they all made for simplification, because the Negro, being adaptable, invariably chooses the easiest way. Not only was he handicapped by a primitive mentality but by differences of physical structure as well. His thick lips and unaccustomed tongue made it impossible for him to pronounce certain vowels, so he merely substituted other sounds that were easier for him. The rolled French *r* was quite beyond his powers, so he "just paid it no never mind" and said *nèg* instead of *nègre,* and *vend* for *vendre.* Only the salient syllables of a word stuck in his memory, so he ruthlessly pruned the first and last ones whenever he could.

Grammar suffered a like drastic simplification. Whenever he was able to make himself understood without the use of a verb, he omitted it entirely and, like an ailing child who whimpers "me sick," he said *moin malade.* He worked out a verb form, relying mostly on the past participle, that was so rudimentary and other modifications so drastic that philologists have classified the Creole dialect, as a separate and distinct language.

Not all the Creole expressions that sound peculiar to modern French ears, however, are attributable to an ignorant mutilation of the language, for some at least are archaic words of the Saintonge or Picardy patois that the slaves learned from their European masters and handed down from generation to generation, long after they had been forgotten in France.

This Creole Dialect is of particular interest to philologists, for the incubation of this weird jargon paralleled at every point the birth of the French language. Just as the clumsy efforts of the semibarbarous Gallic tribes to master the speech of their highly civilized Roman conquerors gave rise to the bastard, lacerated Latin that finally came to be called French; so the attempts of these aboriginal blacks to acquire the idiom of their owners produced the Creole Dialect.

Although every character that darts, ant-wise, in and out of the pages of this book must have spoken Creole, the authors, for the sake of a larger audience, have wisely chosen to write in Standard French, pimented with a few Creole words for indigenous flavor. For this reason the translator has used colloquial English without making any effort to transpose the text into American Negro dialect. The many songs in Creole, however, have been reproduced as written, for, although without literary merit, they have great interest from the point of view of folklore and philology. They are tiringly repetitive, so the translator has merely inserted a line or two of his own to suggest their meaning.

Haiti has suffered at the hands of some travel-writers, who have overemphasized certain of her more sensational aspects with an eye to box-office receipts. Others have painted her in a fair and objective manner; but all have shown us Haiti as she appeared to foreign eyes. In *Canapé-Vert* we have, for the first time in English, a vivid and accurate picture of life on the island seen from the inside. The authors, both Haitian born, have captured the true subtlety of the Negro-peasant mentality, with all its strange, naïve reasoning, its deep-rooted superstition, and the tang and savor of its humor. Indeed it is so authentic and detailed that it might serve as an excellent sociological record of Haitian rural life. This aspect, however, has in no way detracted from the charm and interest of the story, for the situations have been handled with dramatic skill and the characters have been completely humanized.

Canapé-Vert not only gives a true understanding of Haiti and her problems but—even more important in this era of intercontinental rapprochement—an honest sympathy for the difficulties with which she is confronted.

EDWARD LAROCQUE TINKER

CANAPÉ-VERT

CANAPÉ-VERT

CHAPTER I

IT was evening. Flocks of whistling blackbirds, leaving the eastern heights for the mangroves of the bay, crossed the sky. The heat lessened with the first ruffles of the breeze and already darkness was falling in the creases of the hills. Only a single, feeble ray of light still touched the sides of Canapé-Vert. Aladin was returning from his garden where he had spent the afternoon weeding. He washed his face and feet; and then, dragging out a heavy, straw-bottomed chair, prepared to enjoy the coolness of the vine-covered arbor that shaded the entrance to his cabin. He did this every night, waiting for his dinner to be brought, which varied little; a thin porridge of ground corn or a broth of congo peas.

He was a Negro of good stock, a hard worker with a head full of common sense. At the death of his father, who left him a small heritage of two parcels of land and a little money to sustain them, he was in no hurry to set himself up in life, but took a humble mistress called Sanite who lived near his cabin. She was a simple washerwoman, unattached, who took care of Aladin's household. In return he shared his pleasures with her and, whenever necessary, thrashed her, especially Saturday nights when he came home late from a dance and had too much to drink. As he didn't love her, he gave her a fixed sum each week as one would to a servant. But for five years, for want of a better, she had served his purpose. Now he was thinking of taking up with a respectable young girl called Florina. She was nearly sixteen and he, close to thirty, had seen her grow up. Sometimes this difference in age worried him very much because he was sure that people would cackle about it; still it wasn't his fault.

One morning as he went to the well of Jecrois for water, Florina stopped at his door for a bit of gossip with him. The next day, as he had business in Bourdon, he walked as far as the well with her. As for the other days . . . The adventure never ceased to surprise him. "Ay yaie yaie!" exclaimed Aladin that night, smiling in admiration. "Some woman!"

He took up his pipe mechanically and felt in his pockets; he had no more tobacco. He began a humorous gesture but suppressed it, remembering that Sanite would soon bring him his dinner, and he could send her to buy cigarettes at Sor Mélie's. In the meantime he pulled on his empty pipe to give himself the illusion of smoking.

As he daydreamed night had fallen and in weary hopelessness was blanketing the neighboring cabins where lamps were already blinking. It also weighted Aladin's eyes, and the penetrating freshness of the soft breeze made him drowsy. He soon, however, returned to his amorous memories, and ever since the first morning Florina had stopped by his door to chatter with him, he could recall many. Every one was dear to him, even the most insignificant,—a mango she had bitten and given him, a friendly intonation, or a simple farewell smile,—but there was one that particularly agitated him and haunted him more often than the rest. Nevertheless he couldn't quite remember how it had all happened. It was the day that no one was at the well. Florina had just put her calabash under the bamboo spout and was watching it in silence. How did she find herself in his arms, face to face, breath to breath? How had he pulled her to his breast, excited and passionate?—he had never known. Without a cry, not wishing to awake from that violent sweetness, she had closed her eyes and did not repulse him until he tried to throw her on the ferns of the bank.

"Let me go, Aladin," she begged, "let me go. Don't you hear people coming?"

It wasn't true. But he had already released her before he realized it, and the heat of his passion was over. He murmured humbly, "What would you say, Florina, if I was to ask you to live with me?"

She didn't answer, but seized her calabash with pretended brusqueness and turned her back on him. Not knowing exactly what she meant, he drew near to her anxiously.

"Oh, Florina," he said gently.

No response.

"Florina, it's serious what I said to you."

"All right, then," she said finally. "If it's so serious, why don't you go see Grande Da?" Then leaping the embankment at one bound, she ran away.

It was a lovely memory, and he liked to think of it even more because of the vexatious sequel of worries that followed it. First there was the visit to her grandmother—an ancient Negress, gaunt and imperious, with a pipe always hanging from the corner of her mouth. When, in a roundabout way, he confided his desire to start housekeeping with her granddaughter, Grande Da had made a discreet allusion to Sanite. "A dog has four feet," she said, "but he can't run down four roads at the same time." He had let it be understood that his affair with Sanite was a small matter and that he meant to leave her as soon as possible, but although he had taxed his wits to find reasons for a quarrel, he hadn't found a decent excuse for breaking with her. Sanite knew perfectly what he was trying to do and stoically accepted all the mean treatment he chose to inflict, so Aladin, not able to repress a feeling that he was ungrateful, each day put off the final break.

This painful situation had already dragged out for a long month when the price of produce fell so low that he was forced to abandon his idea of setting up housekeeping with Florina for the present. Worries pursued him, one after the other, without end, until he began to think it wasn't natural for a man to be so pestered. So that night, after carefully considering the situation, he decided to force his destiny by striking a hard blow. And as he had finally persuaded himself that all his bad luck was due to Sanite, he resolved to finish with her then and there. Had he not found a charm hidden in his matting?—two needles bound eye to point with thread.

In a little while she came with his dinner, and he began to upbraid her cruelly, pretending without just cause that she was late. Sanite did not reply, but served him submissively as usual—an attitude that instead of placating Aladin only increased his ill humor.

"I'm fed up with you!" he exclaimed harshly. "I'm tired! Tired! . . . Don't you understand that, no?"

She looked at him sadly, and unluckily for her, she appeared all the uglier and was conscious of the cruel way he was aware of it, but he did not insult her, this time. She wanted to tell him that he wasn't good-looking either with his face peppered with pock-marks, but realizing the uselessness of it all, she sighed and said:

"Thank you, Aladin. In spite of all I've done for you, today you think I'm nothing. Very well. I'll go . . . you don't have to chase me away like a dog. Yes, I'll go, since you want it that way, but don't forget what the proverb says, 'the best food is cooked in the old pots.' " She wrung her hands trying hard not to cry.

"It's true," said Aladin with a malicious smile. "The words do say that. But all the old pots aren't alike."

Sanite bit her lips, they were trembling convulsively.

"That's so, that's so! You are right. But the word also says 'pretty woman, much unhappiness.' "

This was a covert allusion to Florina and for nothing in the world would he tolerate that.

"How do you dare to talk like that?" he shouted, exasperated. "Didn't you say you were going? The door's wide open. What are you waiting for?"

The woman bowed her head slowly, and with heavy feet shuffled away.

Florina sighed. The lizards and crickets shook their

tiny rattles incessantly in the cool shadows outdoors. The night invited rest after a grueling day of sun and toil. Prévilon, the young girl's father, unrolled a thick matting of rush and banana stems, and lay down. His wife, Lamercie, came and sat by his pallet and began to clean his ear with a chicken feather. Leaning against the door frame, Florina awaited Aladin's visit, even though she knew she could no longer hope for it—for he never came after eight o'clock. A strange sadness engulfed her—always a premonition of bad luck. But what could weak human beings do against the decrees of fate? Evidently nothing!

Absent-mindedly she watched her grandmother pacing back and forth under the arbor, muttering confused syllables. Why was she striding like that? It would be so much easier to do nothing and drift with the tide. She wanted to stop the old woman but she was afraid to disturb her. When she walked like that she communed with the loas, the spirits of the dead of her family; and often Grande Erzilie, the Vodun divinity, took advantage of these opportunities to enter into her body and possess her. It would have been a sacrilege to disturb her; God knows what misfortunes would have befallen Florina—the least would surely have been a sound beating, for her grandmother never joked in matters that concerned the mystères, or spirits. It was too late now anyway, for the old woman was already humming one of the songs that Grande Erzilie liked best:

"Moin pas gagnin chance, mes amis ô,
Moin pas gagnin chance!
Moin pas gagnin chance, mes amis ô,
Moin pas gagnin chance!
Gnou sèle ti pitite moin gagnin,
L'allé navigué lan la-mè.
Canote chaviré avec li!
Lan la-mè, canote chaviré!"

Her voice got louder and louder, and she chanted her plaint so sorrowfully that it wrenched Florina's heart. Without thinking what she was doing she joined in her grandmother's singing. Finally they both stopped, the old woman ceased her pacing, and extending her arms like a cross, she shouted:

"Moin pas gagnin chance, mes amis ô,
Moin pas gagnin chance!"

As she was about to begin again her frenzied pacing, backward and forward, she wavered and fell to the ground, her body twisting spasmodically. Prévilon hurried quickly to her side, untied the handkerchief on her head, and with deep solicitude, not unmixed with fear, wiped her face. But she fought him off violently.

"Hé! . . . Hé! . . . Hé! . . . Hé! . . . Hé! . . ." she cried savagely, pushing him aside with brutal strength and jumping to her feet.

"It's me, Grande! It's me!" And in truth it was Grande Erzilie Fréda Dahomey speaking through the mouth of Grande Da whose body she had borrowed. Prévilon, Lamercie, and Florina rushed to greet her, in turn prostrating themselves at her feet, and kissing the earth three times. Taking them by the hand she raised them up, making them pivot slowly—one turn to the left, one turn to the right, and again one turn to the left—and all with bows and steps so complicated that one would have said it was a real dance. The salutations finished, they offered her orgeat and rose water, which she accepted coquettishly, but before she drank the orgeat she made the customary three libations, and then perfumed herself generously.

"Thank you, my dear child," she said at last, giving the flask of scent to Florina. "Thank you, my children." And as though to emphasize her gratification, she smiled at them gently with real Creole mischievousness. Then she walked slowly away from them under the arbor, making grandiose gestures, as if she were speaking to herself. From time to time she stopped, crossed her hands behind her back and tossed her head. Her "children," preys to their sacred fear, watched her in silence for they knew she was about to speak and they didn't know what she would reveal to them: good or bad news?

At last she turned to Prévilon, "My son, your affairs go badly. You promised me never to gamble any more; but night before last you lost ten gourdes at dice. You promised me never to drink again, but Saturday you were drunk. Is that any way to behave?"

"That's true, Grande," he answered contritely. "That's true, that! I can't lie to you. But you must know that a bad mystère forced me to do it."

The old woman shook a menacing finger at him. "Listen, Prévilon, listen to me well. I'm going to tell you something; when a man doesn't know how to keep his word, I wash my hands of his affairs. . . . You think a bad spirit pursues you? It makes you gamble in spite of my orders? It makes you drink? It is no such thing. You find pleasure in it! Now me, I warn you once for all. Straighten out your dealings with me. If not, the worse for you! Someday you'll know I'm right."

To tell the truth Prévilon had wanted to consult Grande Erzilie many times, and tell her his troubles, but he had never had enough money to pay for it. His bad angel always got ahead of him and involved him in extravagance, but how could one tell that to Grande Erzilie? Already the old woman had begun to march up and down again, but this time muttering African words—un-understandable. She spoke the ceremonial tongue, "language" as they called it. Florina never took her eyes off her, for she was troubled, having had a strange dream the night before. She had seen herself pushed into a large hole of dirty water with a young stranger who tried in vain to help her. . . . In the morning she had told her dream to her grandmother, the old woman's face had become somber. "Bad dream," she said, "my little one!" Florina closed her eyes, shuddering. When she opened them Grande was planted before her.

"Oh! Florina," said Erzilie. "I see bad things for you. It is the evil loas that will bring this misery upon you. You might escape it if you invoke some powerful mystères. But, aye yaie, yaie! My child! I see misfortunes for you. I see death!"

Something had happened to Florina. She was beyond anguish. She neither saw nor understood anything more. Her ears buzzed and her heart stopped beating. She had to lean against the wall of the cottage to keep from falling. Grande Erzilie continued to talk for a long time. She said all the bad luck affecting the people of Canapé-Vert was due to Tonton Bossa, her sister's husband, who having made a pact with the devils had given them his three sons— Vital, Exanthus, and Philoxène. But, she added, Damballa Oueddo, the master of heaven, was very angry with him. For her part she would keep her eyes open for the welfare of her children. Besides, they would not have to wait long for news of Papa Damballa.

To show how terrible would be his vengeance she shook her fist toward Tonton Bossa's house, menacingly, and cried "Hé! Hé! Hé! Hé!" Then she spun around and fell like a huge tree struck by lightning. Prévilon carried his mother's body into the house to her pallet, and wiped off her face with cool water.

The tenseness of the situation slowly relaxed. Little gusts of air penetrated the house with the thousand small noises that make the peace of rural nights, and dominating the little concert of insects and plants, the small green lizards blew on their straw flutes. . . . When the old woman regained consciousness she asked in a feeble voice:

"What happened to me?"

"Nothing, mother," replied Prévilon calmly.

"You think so, my son! My body is so bruised that it seems as if a mystère had ridden me. . . . Could it have been Grande Erzilie?"

"Yes, mother, she herself!"

"Ah! Grande came! And what did she say?"

"Misfortune dogs us all in Canapé-Vert; Papa Damballa is not content." Then ignoring the reproaches heaped upon him for his own bad conduct, he hurried to add, "According to what Grande says, Tonton Bossa has made some very evil promises."

"It's like that," groaned the old woman. She drew a long deep breath and almost immediately went to sleep, exhausted by the strain of her experience. Prévilon closed the door gently. The family stretched out on their mats, and soon after the lamp was extinguished loud snores filled the hut. The moon came out. . . .

Everyone in the village had suspected Tonton Bossa's evil ways. Did they lose a parent, a cow, or a goat, there was no hesitation in holding him responsible; but as he was a rich and powerful bocor, or sorcerer, no one dared to speak out loud. Only Madan Bossa had had the courage to face her man. Ever since the disappearance of Exanthus she had lived in a little dilapidated toolhouse full of sacks and harness for the work animals. She never closed her eyes the night through. All the time she turned and twisted in the mustiness of soiled clothes and wretchedness, for her improvised bed was a matting of palm spread over boxes and softened, for better or worse, by rags of dresses and men's pants.

Each night at twelve, a great white owl came and perched on a mango tree near the hovel. Three times it hooted and then flew away, like an envoy who had delivered his message and hurried to return to his master—and certainly there could be no doubt that this malevolent bird was a "messenger." At times she heard strange noises. She'd sit up in her pallet and listen; only the rats running over the thatched roof, or some starving dog foraging in the yard for an impossible bone, or perhaps a neighboring donkey that had broken its tether. Then she'd stretch herself out again to be disturbed at some distant barking, the too-human cry of cats in heat, the chafing of trees under the weight of the wind, the plaint of a banana stalk forcing its way up through the earth.

That night the devils had assumed repulsive, bat-like forms, darting untiringly through the hut, whispering and chittering. Vainly she tried to chase them out with a broom. "Your children are not worse than that," they said to her. "Exanthus and Vital are on Mount Gaô. They're working the high ground for us. As for Philoxène, if we've left you his body, we've taken his soul forever."

"Abonochio! abonochio, madichon!" (ab renuncio, ab renuncio, malediction!) screamed Madan Bossa, spitting on the floor.

But the devils burst into laughter, and flitted in circles, hissing their words of evil omen: "They belong to us, to us until the end of centuries. It's Tonton Bossa who gave them to us."

The poor woman continued to cry, "Abonochio! abonochio! madichon!" And the devils answered, "It was your man who gave them to us. He owed us a debt. He paid it."

At last, despairing of chasing them out with her broom or her exorcisms, Madan Bossa changed her tactics. Many times she poured them libations of white rum on the threshold of the door. But the

more the devils drank the more they strove to perse-
cute her. "It was Tonton Bossa who gave them to
us," they repeated without end. "He owed us, so how
could he refuse to pay."

Finally exhausted, resigned to her torment, she lay
down and rolled herself up in a ball like a dog. The
devils wearied too, and no sooner had they left than
a small soft voice like that of her sister, Grande Da,
soothed her as in old times when she was a little girl.

"Cà qui tiré, cà qui tiré, cà qui tiré?
Cà qui tiré, là-à, lan Montagne Gaô?
Cà qui tiré, cà qui tiré, cà qui tiré?
Cà qui tiré, là-à, lan Montagne Gaô?

"Cé moin-même, Oli-Olan!
Coq chanté; coquioco!
Cé moin-même, Oli-Olan!
Coq chanté; coquioco!

"M'a ménin-ou allé lan Montagne Gaô.
M'a ménin-ou allé là-à, lan Montagne Gaô."

"I'll take you to Mount Gaô
I'll take you there, to Mount Gaô."
(supposed to be the home of the spirits.)

What did they want her to know by that? Why
did they imitate the voice of her sister? She didn't

know, but in listening to that song everything seemed to be better. What relaxation! What peace! What growing sweetness! It was as if a thorn of suffering had been plucked from her very being. She was transplanted into a miraculous world where evil never entered. Everything now seemed just and right to her.

This false enchantment lasted until the dawn.

CHAPTER II

WHEN Madan Bossa woke
up daylight was already filtering through the cracks
in the door. She washed her face, quickly slipped on
her shift and left the hovel to take the hill trail that
led to her sister's house. The sun had risen above the
horizon, bathing the summit of Canapé-Vert in a
tender rosy light; the trees, the planted fields, and
the mountains were awakening to happy life—freed
of the night's anxieties, the birds celebrated the coming of day. It was the diurnal rebirth of the world's
youth. The fresh odor of the countryside recaptured
the primeval innocence of ancestral Guinea. And as
if joy must always shine for them through a smoky
screen of nostalgia, some young men on their way

to the coumbite, or harvesting bee, of Ti-Dan, sang
this hymn to the sun in strong tones that were also
plaintive.

"Soleil ô! ati dan Ibo Loco! Soleil ô!
Soleil ô! ati dan Ibo Loco! Soleil ô!

Papa, moin pas moun icite.
Atchango, moin sôti loin,
Soleil ô!

"Papa, m'pas te vin' pou rété.
Ato m'pas cab' travèse.
Soleil ô!"

Thus it was that their voices, rising in unison in
the fresh quiet air, inspired them with the old hope
of the San Domingan slaves that they would return
to Africa after death. This song had survived a century of liberty, for each generation transmitted it
to the one that followed, and these young blacks of
Canapé-Vert sang it with the fervor of their ancestors, just as if they still clung tenaciously to the land
of their origin.

Madan Bossa plodded between the plantings of
corn that glazed the hillside. Sorrow had faded and
withered her before her time. Doubtless her courage
sustained her, for she was entirely immersed in the
misfortunes of her children. The beauty of the world

was not for her, nor the songs of man, nor the light
of God. Nothing survived in her heart but the stabbing thought that her sons were toiling in the accursed lands where no Christians go, and where the
mysterious voice had promised to lead her. . . .

"Ho—ho!" she said, trembling. She suddenly realized that that voice could be none other than the
devil's. "But yes, it was an evil spirit that sang that
song." She spat three times in the direction of Tonton Bossa's house.

"May the hand of my man, the left hand to be
sure, be no stranger to the curse that follows the
family." She realized the truth of it all now. Everything that had seemed to her inexplicable and without significance was suddenly clarified and took on
precise meaning.

On a stormy October night, two years ago, just
before All Saints' Day, when it was wise to take precautions against Baron Samedi—the Vodun god of
the cemetery—two white Americans came to Tonton
Bossa with little black boxes to take pictures. As
they couldn't speak Creole, they explained by signs
that they were lost, and Tonton Bossa willingly sent
his oldest son, Vital, to put them on the right
road . . . He never came back. Quickly the rumor
spread that the white men, who now and then have
strange vices, had killed poor little Vital and buried
him somewhere in a thicket. Good! But wasn't it just
a year later, day for day, that Philoxène disappeared

in his turn under circumstances that were just as strange; and within a few months a Negro of the hills, returning from town, met him standing in the middle of the path like a ghost! The man asked him to let him pass but, getting no answer, he looked at the child and saw that his eyes were fixed and glassy like a corpse. He was so upset that he cried in terror and ran away. Aroused by the noise the neighbors went to the place, recognized Philoxène, and brought him back to his parents. Bon! But it was not a living Christian who was returned to them—it was a zombi, a body without a soul, a flesh and bone phantom that ate, drank, did everything it was ordered to do but could not speak or think. . . .

During this time Tonton Bossa's affairs had prospered considerably. Everything he undertook succeeded, and so well, indeed, that only fools could believe it was by chance. Thus in these bad times, in spite of poor prices, he had built three lime kilns. His friends, sure that he was committing a folly, did all they could to dissuade him, but he shook his head like an obstinate old Negro and would not listen to them. To the great surprise of the people of Canapé-Vert he fired his furnaces one after the other without being able to fill all of his orders. Also, in no time at all, he had become the richest man of the section. His ambitions seemed at last satisfied. He even built on his wife's land, on the top of the hill, a new houm-for, with a peristyle roofed with tin, that was much more elaborate than the old one, and he proposed to consecrate it, ostentatiously, after the corn had been harvested.

Bon! But wasn't it also true that during this time he delivered little Exanthus to his demons? Madan Bossa knitted her brows, "Aye, papa!" she murmured in a low voice. "God is my witness, once, twice, three times, you will someday have to pay me for that." At last she reached the big road. At the turn before her sister's house she met Florina who was going for water to Jecrois spring with a gourd under her arm.

"Good morning, aunt," said the young girl.

"Good morning, little one," replied Madan Bossa without slackening her pace. "Has Grande Da gone down to the garden yet?"

"No! Aunty," Florina called back, "I'm going to the spring," and she continued on her way swaying her supple, slender body like a lazy branch.

Under the arbor of lush green vines that covered the door Grande Da was dripping coffee. For the last time, in order to save every drop, she shook the little cloth bag, browned by use, over the pot that bubbled on a fire of faggots. Prévilon, patiently waiting, squatted not far from his mother and tapped the floor with his pruning knife, while Lamercie, to drive out the bad night air, sprinkled the threshold with eau-repugnance. Everything was calm. The first duties of the day were finished. But when Madan

Bossa entered the yard it was like a gust of wind.
Grande Da raised her head.

"Oh! Sor Cicie!" she said, surprised. "What brings
you here so early in the morning?"

"What brings me? . . . Why, sister, don't you
know what happened at our house? . . . The devils
came to see me last night and told me everything!"
Madan Bossa shut her eyes and shook her head; then
as if to vent her feelings, she made angry gestures,
tapping her foot and making her whole body tremble.

"Sit down if you want to talk," said Grande Da,
pointing to a chair.

Madan Bossa seated herself with a sigh. At last
she said, "Sister, you see Bossa," she made a face and
spat. "He isn't a man, no, he's a demon!"

"Don't say that, Sor Cicie!'

"Ho—ho! I tell you. . . . It's all very well that he
has a nose, eyes, a mouth, like everybody else; but
it's a devil that he is. Yes!"

"Enough!" Grande Da ordered, putting her hands
before her eyes.

But Madan Bossa went on. "Ever since that day
when Exanthus disappeared my heart has been so
filled with trouble that I have slept all alone in the
little hut in the rear of the yard."

"Like that!" replied Grande Da surprised.

"What would you have done in my place? When
a man mixes in evil matters, can one ever know how
one stands with him? Besides, what you have just

heard is still nothing. In the night when that man thought I was asleep, he would get up quietly, go to the door and begin to talk as if he had someone with him. He talked, and talked, and talked!"

"Hooo!" exclaimed Grande Da in alarm. "What's that you tell me, Sor Cicie?"

"Well, if he wasn't talking with the devils you tell me who he was talking with!"

"Do you know about this?" Lamercie gave a long sigh. Prévilon bowed his head and tapped the ground again with his pruning knife.

"Ever since I've been sleeping in that little hut," continued Madan Bossa, "an owl comes to perch all night on the mango tree."

"Would you believe it!"

"It hoots three times and then flies away."

"It must be that it comes to tell you something."

"That's what I thought too in the beginning. But it was only yesterday that I managed to discover the real truth. . . . Sister, is your door well closed? Do you think the bats can get in here?"

"Oh! no, no! That is impossible."

"All right. Good! Last night my eyes were full of sleep. I lay down and then I felt just as if someone was telling me not to go to sleep."

"Sis—ter!"

"I turned first on my right side, and then on my left; ho—ho! One would say that the thing was keeping my eyes from closing. And then, what do you think I saw? A bat that was flying in my room."

"And your door was well-closed?"

"My door was tight shut, sister!"

"My God!" exclaimed Grande Da. And, as if to call on the others as witnesses, she asked them, "Did you hear that?"

"Then I got up," continued Madan Bossa. "I lit my lamp, I opened the door, and then I seized a big broom to chase the evil spirits out. Ho—ho! here comes another. And then one more! It was as light as day . . . Tell me, sister, did you ever hear of bats coming into the light?"

"Oh! No. No! That's never been known."

"That's what I said too. . . . Then I took a bottle of rum, I went to the door, I poured them a stiff drink. Ho—ho! It was then that they began to fly around. One moment one would brush my head with its wings, another second it would be my shoulder. Then it began to talk."

"Wasn't that awful! Ro-o-oh!"

"They told me that Tonton Bossa had made a compact to give them my children!" She sobbed convulsively. Then she stammered in a low smothered voice, "They carried them off to Mount Gâo, where they are working for the devils."

A heavy, long silence followed Sor Cicie's words. Looking afar off, Grande Da appeared to be thinking. The others, disquieted, refused to meet each other's eyes. At last Prévilon made up his mind to talk. The simplicity of his spirit gave a certain authority to his opinions, and this gave him assurance. The words of the simple-minded, are they not those of God?

"Aunty," began Prévilon. "I'm a child of yesterday morning, that's true. When grown-up people speak, children don't enter into the conversation, isn't that so? Still there are times when the aged listen to children, for they too have wise words. Aunty, what I am going to say is something worth looking into. Suppose that there is a great tree in your yard. Under the tree you plant peas. But the tree has many leaves. When the sun warms the earth, its light does not reach the peas. Don't your peas have to die? Good, you want to save them. Mustn't you put the ax to the tree? Oughtn't you to cut it to the ground? If you don't want to do it, then you must lose your peas! . . ."

Grande Da interrupted Prévilon with a gesture of her hand.

"Sor Cicie, Damballa is your guardian spirit, isn't that right? When you are in trouble, isn't it him that you call upon? Doesn't he tell you what you must do? What Prévilon has said is good. I won't deny it. But me, in your place, I would tell all the family. That is what I advise you to do. We'll come to your house. We'll call Damballa. And what must be done, he will do."

"You are right," said Madan Bossa. "We will call all the family to my house."

Suddenly a burst of laughter from behind the cactus hedge on the big road startled them. It was the voice of Florina who seemed to have already forgotten the gloomy predictions of Grande Erzilie. She came in followed by Aladin. The young man saluted them timidly, touching the rim of his hat. "Han!" said he, smiling. "Good morning, monsieur—dames."

"Good morning, Aladin," they replied without cordiality.

"It was when I was coming back that I met him," Florina hastened to explain. "He was returning from Moronvil where he'd been to see a little pig that Bobo is raising for him." Uncomfortable because of her grandmother's severe expression, she didn't dare go on with her story. Meekly, she went into the house, put down her water-gourd in a dark, cool corner, and offered Aladin a chair.

"Now, my friends," said Madan Bossa. "I'm leaving. I have a little errand to do. When I've finished it I will go and notify all my relatives. Then it will be tomorrow, Thursday, Damballa Oueddo's sacred day. . . . I'll have to have everything ready for the service by this afternoon. . . ."

"Good," approved Grande Da. "Won't you have a little cup of coffee before you go?"

"No, sister, my heart's too heavy."

"And you, Aladin?"

"Han! Yes, please," he answered awkwardly. Finishing it hurriedly, he bent toward Florina and whispered to her, "This afternoon, I can't go down to
the spring with you. I've got to go to my compère's,
Ti-Dan. But this evening, God willing, I'll come to
see you."

"True?" she said to him in a caressing voice. "True,
Aladin? You won't do what you did last night? I'll
wait for you if you mean it."

"Once I've promised you, Florina," replied Aladin
in a reproachful tone, "I'll keep my word." Then he
said good-bye and hurried after Madan Bossa down
the hill.

CHAPTER III

IT WAS the beginning of
the hot months, and the drying bushes exhaled a pep-
pery scent of wild flowers. Already the sun weighed
heavily upon the earth. Slowly, the valley of Bourdon, where the last mangoes were ripening, emerged
from the thick shadow of the hills, and the island of
Gonave detached itself from the murky horizon at
the farther end of Port-au-Prince bay.

With rolling hips and swinging arms, Madan Bossa
measured the countryside with long strides. Behind
her came Aladin, heavy with coffee and his dreams of
love, who had trouble in keeping up with her. From
time to time a dove cooed, a quail whistled, and
in the vast silence of the country the calls took on

the friendly color of salutations. But the two people traveled on, indifferent to the outside world; Aladin thinking of Florina, and Madan Bossa going over the names of those she should invite to the ceremony. When she was about to leave Aladin, she turned toward him and said, "I'm counting on you to let Sor Mélie know that I expect her tomorrow."

"Of course I'll carry your message."

"Thank you, my son. I'm going now." And she entered the narrow path that twisted to her dwelling.

Freed of the necessity of keeping up with the nervous pace of Cicie, Aladin slowed his gait and dawdled along his journey, no longer glancing to right and left for fear of stepping on a thorn with his naked feet, or bruising them against the stones. Now he could see his garden and his tiny house surrounded with coffee and banana trees; a little lower the fields of Ti-Dan which his friends were working—singing all the while. But Aladin was thinking of the future, of Florina. . . . She smelled of the good, damp earth, that child of God who had surely fashioned her with his own hands. It pleased him to imagine she had sprung up in a single night, like thin stems of bamboo, at first tender and then hardening in the light, until she became that miraculous being with hips, stomach, buttocks, breasts, and those large, shining, liquid eyes! A Negress without her equal in beauty, in courage, made for love as for maternity and all work, and who promised a happy destiny for

the man who could make her enter his house. Truly
Aladin could boast that he had found a prize. He
smiled at his thought, and was filled with great
benevolence toward everything. Words began to
group themselves in his mind until his happiness burst
out in song:

> "La-Rousée!
> M'pr'al' taillé chimin-moin
> Pou m'pas mouillé. . . ."

> "Rose!
> I will trim the branches along your path,
> So you will not get wet."

A startled lizard ran between his feet; nimbly
he avoided it, content not to crush it. And in his
mood he would have saved with the same solicitude
even the most venomous of little beasts—a scorpion,
a spider crab, a centipede. . . .

He stopped at the cemetery, and among the tombs
sown here and there in the wild grass, he bowed his
head, recited a short prayer, and continued on his
way. At length he passed his own door and hurrying
around a turn in the road reached Sister Mélie's door.
"Good morning, everybody," said he.

"Good morning, Aladin," they replied.

Taking his greasy felt hat off, he folded it carefully, placed it on a big stone and sat down on it.

Sister Mélie's store had something of an air—an old
house with lizard-tracked walls under its sheet-iron
roof that made it unique in the quarter. It was the
rendezvous of all the best young people of Canapé-
Vert. It was, to be sure, the only store in that vicinity,
but the sympathetic welcome of its owner attracted
many customers. Besides, if one were a little hard up,
Sister Mélie never refused a small credit of two or
three gourdes.

That day a dozen people were sitting around without ceremony, some on boxes, others on the threshold
or even on the hard-packed earth of the arbor. A
goblet of absinthe passed from hand to hand, each
one pouring three tiny libations on the ground before
drinking, as they repeated to themselves: "Marassas,
les Saints, les Morts"—the Twins, the Saints, the
Dead. Chatter was going on at a great rate. They
rehashed the gossip of the neighborhood, and spiced
it with proverbs and parables, which flowed in abundance from their sententious lips. . . . When they
had entirely finished with the news of Canapé-Vert,
Aladin, who had not said one word since his arrival,
asked, "Have you heard what's happening on the
other side of the water?"

"But yes!" replied a ruddy, squat little mulatto
with assurance. Then he took a swallow of absinthe,
made a face, and added in a thick voice: "The French
want to fight with the Germans! That's a piece of
news that has been circulating for two days."

"That's what I heard," said another. "But there is one thing I can't understand. Why those whites are always wanting to make war on each other. They must surely have too little to do. Me, if I was the Good Lord, I'd send them a busy itch that would keep them occupied."

"I know why they're ready to fight this time," remarked Aladin, smiling with an air of superiority. Then he went over to light his pipe at the fire where Sister Mélie was cooking a fricassee of codfish for her customers. After he had taken several puffs and clapped his hat on his head, he spat noisily and began to explain matters in his own way.

"Suppose," said he, "that the yard over there is yours and this one is mine. You've got a lot of mangoes; me, I've got a lot of corn. But you, you have many things that I don't possess. Your neighbors give you anything you need; you give them mangoes in return. Me, no one gives me anything. I've only corn, but I also like mangoes. What do I do? I wait until night, then I cross over to your house and I pick me a mess of mangoes. But you are not yet asleep. You hear a noise in your yard; what do you do? You get up, you take your machete, you go out, you run into me and you attack me. My son, who hears this, comes with his machete and attacks you in turn. And so here come all your neighbors to rescue you; while my son's friends arrive too. Now you tell me, isn't that war?"

"But yes, true."

"Well! That's the same way things happen on the other side of the water."

"Ah, Aladin, that's true! that's true! OH! Oh! Oh! That's right. That's so! What a man!" they exclaimed.

Aladin got up, full of gravity and condescension. He touched the brim of his hat. "Pardon me," he said and departed.

He had hardly gone a few steps on the road when Sister Mélie ran after him, crying noisily, "Oh Aladin! When will you give me the money you owe me?" But when she got closer to him, she whispered in a low voice, "Sanite told me you had left her. . . . I never thought you'd do her like that. . . . But let that go! It's Florina, hein! who ought to be contented? What a lucky child! Hardly has she begun life when she finds a brave boy like you to go crazy about her! . . ." Aladin was uncomfortable, so Sister Mélie smiling maliciously, hastened to change the subject, "Aladin! didn't someone tell me that Tonton Bossa's Exanthus had disappeared?"

"That's what I heard, I too, Sor Mélie."

"What's it all about, Aladin? Everyone's talking about it. Yes."

"Aye! Sor Mélie. And Tonton Bossa isn't a child

of yesterday morning, oh no. But now I think of it, I came to tell you that Madan Bossa is having a little service tomorrow afternoon. I almost forgot to say she expects you. It has to do with the disappearance of Exanthus. They're going to call up Damballa Oueddo, to see what he can do for the family. . . . I didn't mean to interrupt you. Did you have more to say?"

Sister Mélie looked around, distrustfully, and said, in a low voice, "Ti-Dan told me right out that the other night, after the Danse Congo of Démossié, he was going home. At the crossroads where the mapou tree stands, he met a huge pig . . ." She spread her arms. "This big! Ti-Dan wanted to pass; but the dirty beast wouldn't budge!"

"Don't tell me, Sor Mélie!"

"Ho-ho! I'm telling you!"

"Just like that!"

"But luckily Ti-Dan, as you know, is never without his dogberry stick. He struck it on the ground three times, and then recited the right prayer. . . . Wasn't he obliged to go round by Zinzin's to get home? . . . Why should those people employ evil spirits like that? You tell me if Tonton Bossa hasn't a curse on him?"

Aladin pulled his hat over his forehead and scratched the back of his head. "Sor Mélie," said he, "when you hear the strokes of midnight I don't ad-

vise you to look out at the hill. The old ones said
that always brought bad luck."

"I know that too, Aladin."

"Then," said he with an embarrassed air, "then.
. . . Sor Mélie, I haven't told you anything. No!"

Mélie smiled slyly. "Good-bye, Aladin," she called
in a loud voice. "You'll bring me the money Saturday. . . ."

When Aladin arrived at Ti-Dan's to lend his help
at the planting, as a good neighbor should, the coumbite was nearly finished. His friends jeered him for
being late; they even sang, making flippant allusions
to his flirtation with Florina;

> "Aladin, côté ou té yé?
> Aladin ô, côté ou té yé.
> En-bas codes, mes amis!
> En-bas codes, oh! mes amis!
>
> "Femme, oooh! Femme!
> Rooh!
> Femme, oooh! Femme!
> Rooh!"

But the men were getting hungry and they were
in a hurry to finish the work of potato setting, so
the hoes beat in a strong rhythm, cutting and tear-

ing the soil apart. As the holes were dug, the women
put in the potato eyes and quickly packed the ground
around them with their feet. Since morning there
had been no rest for anyone. They had worked the
soil after it had been cleared of insects and weeds,
by fire. That had been the longest and the hardest
job, and the planting had only begun toward midday. But it seemed as if the men's courage, whipped
by alcohol, grew in proportion to their fatigue. The
work was done while singing, for a couplet was given
by a leader who, as an accompaniment, beat upon
his machete with a little piece of iron, and the metal-
lic sound seemed to electrify them.

> "Planté pois,
> N'apé planté patate, rooh!
> Planté gname,
> N'apé planté patate, rooh!"

The others intoned the chorus in unison;

> "Ah! oh! oh!
> Rooh!
> Ah! oh! oh!
> Rooh!"

Aladin took the leader's place. It was always his
job at the coumbite, and there was not his equal at
improvisation. Ti-Dan never took part in the plant-

ing, for he was the head of the coumbite. He had
no other duties but to act as host and serve his
friends. He watched over the pots and at each demand ran with a bottle of rum. In return everyone
worked for him, and sang his praises:

"Vive chef coumbite-là!
Cé Ti-Dan qui ba nous boué,
Cé Ti-Dan qui ba nous mangé,
Vive chef coumbite-là!

"Ah! oh! oh!
Roooh!
Ah! oh! oh!
Roooh!"

Work came to an end about three in the afternoon. Then the men and the women stretched out
in the shade around the steaming pots. Ti-Dan
served them with a generous hand, and they ate in
silence—potatoes, bananas, malangas, yams, and codfish. Then came the national dish, the traditional peas
and rice cooked with forcemeat balls. There were
many bumpers of rum . . . At last, the repast finished, tongues became loosened, and the matter of
Tonton Bossa naturally came up; the excoriation of
his conduct was unanimous for it might easily bring
horrible misfortunes to the people of Canapé-Vert,
already suffering from hard times, because the bad

spirits always avenged themselves on the innocent
and the guilty alike. . . . Ti-Dan shook his head
gravely, clicked his tongue, and said:

"Now, my friends, ay ayaye! They tell you that it's
the unhappy wretches in the country who are the
meanest. But you know the saying: 'All the animals
of the sea eat human flesh, but only the shark has a
bad name.' Well, I assure you all that when the rich
in the cities handle their affairs, they are hard. They
are very hard."

"Nothing could be truer than what you say there,"
put in Zinzin. "My dead father always taught me
that, and you know he had plenty experience."

"The story I'm going to tell you," continued Ti-
Dan, "I got from Gros-Moceau, last week. You all
know Gros-Moceau, don't you? Mr. Desvallons' tenant farmer?"

"Of course, Ti-Dan, we know him!"

"Well! Gros-Moceau worked Mr. Desvallons' land
well, and Mr. Desvallons was satisfied with him, and
Gros-Moceau was content with Mr. Desvallons. It
was a pleasure to see. They may talk to you of pigs,
cattle, chickens, goats; but it was at Mr. Desvallons'
that all those things were plentiful. As for potatoes,
corn, manioc, ah! It's better to say nothing; you
wouldn't believe the truth. . . . But one day Mr.
Desvallons goes to town and happens to meet Maître
Volny, the notary.

" 'Oh! oh! friend Desvallons, how do you do?'

" 'Things are good enough, and how about you, Volny?'

" 'Me?' The notary shook his head. 'My business brings me nothing.'

"As you know," continued Ti-Dan with his story, "Mr. Desvallons is a very kindhearted man. He's a sympathetic person, so he said to Maître Volny that he ought to leave the city and go into the country to be a farmer."

" 'Does it pay, Desvallons?' "

" 'Yes, it pays! Come up Sunday to my plantation at Musseau. You will see, and you'll tell me whether it pays or not!'

"Well! Maître Volny listened to his friend and went to see how things were up there . . . Ho-ho! he is so interested that he wants a farm right away, he also! So Mr. Desvallons cuts off a piece of his property and lets his friend have it."

"Just like that, Ti-Dan," exclaimed Bobo.

"Just as I say. . . . But when Maître Volny took over the land what do you think he did? He called in Gros-Moceau and, in a roundabout way, began to talk to him about the planting he had done at Mr. Desvallons, and told him he was a good workman. All that in order to find out how much he made. Gros-Moceau told him that in addition to half the crops, Mr. Desvallons paid him ten gourdes a month by way of encouragement. Then Maître Volny looked Gros-Moceau straight in the eye and said, 'If you come to work for me on half shares, I'll give you twenty gourdes.' "

"There you are!" said Zinzin. "Mr. Desvallons asked for it. Doesn't the proverb say that it's the crab's kind heart that keeps it from having a head?"

"That's not all," continued Ti-Dan. "Gros-Moceau refused Volny's dishonest offer. One day Mr. Desvallons calls Gros-Moceau and asks him to do a little weeding for his friend. Hearing this, Gros-Moceau scratched his head and answered, 'Mr. Desvallons, you have too kind a heart. I've got to tell you something; Maître Volny offered me twenty gourdes a month to leave you and work for him.' 'What's that you say, Gros-Moceau? Don't you know Maître Volny is my best friend? You surely must have misunderstood him.' "

"But," said Zinzin, "look at that! Just as I say. Gros-Moceau had no business to mix in the affairs of those people. They don't belong to him."

"Exactly," approved Bobo. "But that's the very reason the poor can never improve their condition. They are too busy guarding the interests of their employers. . . ."

"What you say is very true; but that was not the case with Gros-Moceau," replied Ti-Dan. "Mr. Desvallons treated him fairly. Besides, that's not the whole story. Listen to the rest . . . Bon! Maître Volney begins to have cattle, goats, and pigs in his turn. And as for Mr. Desvallons, he had a good heart,

didn't he, and fine fields. Then what did Maître
Volny do? He let out his beasts one night. They
crossed over to Mr. Desvallons', and the next morning Gros-Moceau saw all his work ruined. He goes
to find his employer; 'Mr. Desvallons! Mr. Desvallons! Come see . . . !' Now I've told you already
that Mr. Desvallons was very sympathetic. Nothing
could be truer, but he had a bad temper, too. When
he saw the destruction to his fields, he took his revolver and killed all his friend's animals. Maître
Volny, who hears this, comes to protest. And it is
only what Mr. Desvallons forgot that day that he
didn't say to him. Since then they're enemies. . . ."

Ti-Dan stopped speaking, lit his pipe, and started
a bottle of rum on the rounds. "I wouldn't be surprised," said he finally, "that someday that affair
would end like that of Jeanlusse and Kinda. Do you
remember that story?"

Surely they remembered it! For the last ten years
they had been talking about it at Canapé-Vert! But,
because it had never ceased to intrigue the people
of the neighborhood, and because it was on that occasion that Tonton Bossa revealed himself in his true
colors, Ti-Dan told it once more to his friends.

"Jeanlusse and Kinda," said he, "were cousins, but
they lived together like two brothers. Kinda couldn't
take a drink if Jeanlusse wasn't with him; when Jeanlusse went to a dance, he always stopped by to pick
up Kinda. . . . In short, it would be impossible to

find people living in greater harmony. But Jeanlusse
had luck. He succeeded in everything he undertook,
while Kinda was the personification of bad luck. If
he got called in to do a little job of work, he was
always sick, and when he was recovered, no one had
any need for him. When it began to rain, it was then
that Kinda didn't have any seeds to plant in the
ground; and when he had corn or millet, the drought
had already begun. Every night, in spite of this,
Jeanlusse went to drink at Kinda's. . . . One good
day, Sor Ti-Ma, Jeanlusse's wife, said to him: 'Listen,
Jeanlusse, you see what bad luck Kinda has, and yet
you are always going to drink at his house. Ayayaye!
my dear, my advice to you is to avoid him, if you
don't want misfortune to fall on you. . . .' But the
man wouldn't listen to her. One night when Ti-Dan
was on the big road he heard screams at Jeanlusse's
and went in to see what had happened. It was poor
Jeanlusse, who had just died of a horrible colic; and
his wife was accusing Kinda of having poisoned him
with a crab soup. Now, just at that moment, as if
by chance, Tonton Bossa came in. 'Sor Ti-Ma,' said
he, 'now that the man is dead all you can do is to
bury him. Screams, tears, or words won't bring him
back.' Then he took her aside and spoke with her for
a long time in a low voice. No one knew what he said
that night. But the next day, before the closing of
the coffin, at a sign from Tonton Bossa, Sor Ti-Ma
addressed the people around her: 'It's the twenty-

third of October, isn't it? Well, my friends, in ten days, on the festival of the dead, you will receive news of me.' After which she placed a cigar in the mouth of the corpse and a bottle of rum near his head, she armed his right hand with a dagger and his left with a stone, saying, 'The cigar is for you to smoke on the way; the bottle of rum to give you courage; the knife so that you can avenge yourself on Kinda, and the stone so you can crush his head. . . .' And it happened that, on the very day fixed by Jeanlusse's wife, Kinda was found murdered in his bed. His chest was pierced like a sieve and his head crushed by a stone. People were astonished; but it wasn't that it seemed extraordinary to them. They had already seen many others such. They couldn't get over the sight of Tonton Bossa, himself, engaged in black sorcery—working with his left hand, as the expression goes."

"Oh! oh! oh!" exclaimed Aladin, just as if he was hearing the tale for the first time in his life. "That was the way of it, Ti-Dan?"

"Just like that, Aladin," affirmed Ti-Dan. "But ever since the day, I've always known that I had to take my precautions with Tonton Bossa."

"As for that!" said Aladin with an evasive air. . . .

CHAPTER IV

Notwithstanding the stifling heat of that June afternoon, Madan Bossa's guests crowded under a huge arbor covered with leaves of the coco palm. As always on holidays, the women wore printed calico dresses and gay neckerchiefs of varied colors and tints, that ran from tender mauve to burning red, through blues, greens, yellows, and pinks. They had shoes, even the poorest who had put on their slippers of sisal, but the men were barefooted, with their trousers rolled up to their knees, their machetes at their sides. They had kept on their working clothes of blue jeans, and the hounsis, or initiates of the Serpent Cult, were clothed and coiffed in ritual white.

Grande Da sat on a low chair in the middle of the assembly. She was straight and majestic, and in her hand she carried the bell and ceremonial calabash ornamented with necklaces of varicolored beads and vertebrae of adders that rattled when they were shaken. She had been chosen, unanimously, to preside over the rites because they knew that, being a proven diplomat, she would avoid any embarrassing incidents between Tonton Bossa and Sister Cicie. In addition she was a mambo, or hereditary Vodun priestess, well-versed in the ritual of the cult, and would conduct the ceremony with understanding so that the mystères, or spirits, in question would not be irritated. And they had made no mistake in selecting her.

At the beginning of the meeting, addressing her brother-in-law, who stood apart near the door of the houmfor, she had made a little speech that had put everyone at their ease. Doubtless Tonton Bossa had looked at her with an enigmatical expression in his eyes, a little trace of malice and something of defiance, but it was only fleeting and one could see that the great calm and courtesy of Grande Da had made an impression upon him.

"Bossa," she said, "we know your misfortune. But the proverb tells us that the goat's business is none of the sheep's. Isn't that so? Nevertheless, suppose that one day the goat falls into trouble, then he should call on the sheep and make a clean breast of everything. Bon! In that case the sheep should give him a little advice. If he is a good neighbor, isn't it his duty to do it? If he does not, isn't he a bad neighbor? But in this affair here, Bossa, neither the goat nor the sheep can say a single word. Each one has his own individual spirit, or loa, as indeed he has everything on God's globe. If you were born, it's because your mystère wanted it so. If it rains so that your peas and your corn grow well, it's your mystère that sends you this blessing. But if some evil spirit cross your path, what can you do against it? The spirit's affairs are the spirit's affairs, and the word tells us also that the unknown is stronger than we are. Now, since Damballa is your mystère, you should call on him for help. Only he can teach you what you must do to escape from this terrible situation."

Thus Grande Da had spoken, and everybody approved of what she said.

It was the moment to open the ceremony. Already those present had clapped their hands and sung the preliminary hymns, "Aizan Dokoué, ô Legba, hé! . . . Papa Legba, open the door for us. . . . Aizan, what is it, what is this, Kéké? . . . etc." Sister Cicie advanced towards the choir of hounsi-bossals—the lowest rank of initiates—and with her arms extended crosswise and nodding her head, she began to sing:

"Ala mauvais pitite moin gagnin!
Li quitté caille Damballah,
L'al' balé caille étranger. . . ."

"Oh! the bad child that I have!
He has deserted the house of Damballa,
He has gone to sweep that of a stranger."

"Abobo! Amen!" cried Grande Da in a brittle, vibrant voice, ringing her small bell sharply. The song in Madan Bossa's throat stopped. Cut short in the middle. And the assistants repeated Abobo! Amen! It was because Sister Cicie made too clear an allusion to the impiety of Tonton Bossa in this chant, which too was modeled on a hymn to Ogoun Badagris.

"Little sister," scolded Grande Da severely, "listen to me well; if you sing any more things like that, I'll leave you in your scrape alone, and let you get out the best way you can. Thanks to God, my friends, I am not a child, me."

Madan Bossa was discouraged. "It isn't my fault that reproach weighs too heavily on my heart. I can't stand any more! I can't stand any more. It is necessary that I tell it!"

Grande Da shrugged her shoulders in disdain at this admission of weakness. For herself, she was strong and her heart had been tempered in the suffering of a whole lifetime. She ordered that a bowl of wheat flour be brought her and then she made her way slowly towards the central support of the arbor where she knelt down. Taking a few pinches of the flour in her hand she traced a large circle on the ground, and other esoteric designs sacred to Damballa Oueddo, made libations of white wine on them, and kissed these symbols where she had sprinkled them. Tonton Bossa, Cicie, Mélie, Aladin, and all the other initiates in their turn performed the same rite. It was doubtless a gesture of humility, and as they got up, their mouths smeared with dirt, they wiped them off, hurriedly, with the backs of their hands. . . .

At last the chants and dances began. As it was in the middle of the week and police regulations forbade drums except on Saturday nights and Sundays, Aladin had to substitute for them, and with tapping foot and hands cupped over his mouth, he did his best to make a suitable accompaniment for the sacred melodies.

"Voum da houm!
Da voum da!
Houm da voum!"

All these chants were used to summon Damballa Oueddo! The most appropriate, in the circumstances, and one that had been asked for by Sister Cicie, was

"Damballah, ô! Signalé ô!
Signalé ô! Maît' moin ô!
Papa Damballah ô!
Signalé ô! Ah-hié ôh!
Rhélé Damballah, oh! Jésus-Mémoi oh!
An-hié, oh! m'souffri assez!
Rhélé Damballah, oh! Jésus-Mémoi, oh!
An-hié, oh! m'souffri assez!
Rhélé Damballah, oh! Jésus-Mémoi, oh!
An-hié, oh! m'souffri assez!
Damballah o! Jésus-Mémoi ô!
M'souffri assez!
Damballah, o! Jésus-Mémoi ô!
M'souffri assez!
Damballah o! Jésus-Mémoi ô!
M'souffri assez!"

"Oh Damballa! Oh Memory of Jesus.
I've suffered enough."

Mimicking the twisting and writhing of a ser-
pent, symbolic of Damballa, the hounsi initiates
danced the yanvalou, while Aladin, aided by the gen-
eral handclapping, carried the song with emphasis.
Voum! . . . Voum! . . . Voum! . . . Voum! . . .
Dada voum! . . .
Voum! . . . Voum! . . . Voum! . . . Voum! . . .
Dada voum! . . .
And the hounsi, with legs and bodies bent, danced

slowly and gravely with their feet and shoulders;
two steps to the right, two steps to the left. . . .

But that day they called on the Master of heaven
in vain! Doubtless offended by the presence of Tonton Bossa, he remained deaf to their supplications
and would not descend among his "children." Nevertheless, he displayed his infinite goodness by returning little Exanthus to his mother.

Towards evening, when the sky had already begun
to grow pale, a confused clamor was heard coming
from the hillside. It grew louder as the crowd approached, like the noise of rain, and soon voices
could be distinguished blended with the tumult of
many footsteps, of stones, and of broken branches.
It happened very quickly. Exanthus appeared suddenly in the yard, escorted by at least thirty natives
all talking at once and very excited.

At the sight of her son, who walked like an au-
tomaton, Madan Bossa trembled violently, and cried
in a voice hoarse and broken:

"Exanthus, my dear little child! What's happened
to make you like that! . . . Bossa, you see him! You
see what you've done to him! . . . Vital and Philoxène! Were they not enough? Aye! Papa Damballa, he sold Exanthus' soul! . . . Aye! . . . Aye!
. . . Aye! . . . Oh Exanthus, what is this trouble?
. . ." She threw herself on the ground, writhing violently.

"Hold her!" ordered Grande Da. Then she raised

her hand to impose silence, for everyone was talking at once, wanting to be the first to know how the child had been found and returned. Speaking to those who had brought him, she demanded, "Who found the child?" It was Zinzin. As he was nearing Madan Bossa's he saw a huge pig coming out of the cemetery. It crossed the road. When he saw Zinzin the pig jumped into the bushes along the path, and almost at the same instant Exanthus came out. . . .

It was a repetition, as anyone could see, of the adventure of Philoxène with the hog. And the people remembered equally well the wicked-looking beast that had barred Ti-Dan's path the other evening. They couldn't restrain their indignation, and now that Tonton Bossa had been unmasked by his own wife, they also dared to make him face the terror he inspired in them. Only Grande Da, in the midst of the general excitement, kept her cool, calm judgment. Approaching the child she spoke gently in his ear, took him by the hand, and led him to the houmfor that housed the shrine of the Vodun gods, where Philoxène had been staying since he was brought back.

At last people began to leave. Sister Mélie, more talkative than ever, took the lead, and when she got out of the yard, feeling herself safe from Grande Da's thunderbolts, manifested her sentiments by singing lustily:

"Ala mauvais pitite moin gagnin!
Li quitté caille Damballah,
L'al' balé caille étranger . . ."

"Behold the ungrateful child I have!
He left the house of Damballa,
To sweep the house of a stranger."

Everyone scattered over the countryside, hurrying
to reach their homes before the downpour foretold
by a rainy wind and black clouds. Night fell suddenly. Already the wood lice and termites, fleeing
their fragile shelters, flew out to find the light. Tonton Bossa withdrew into the houmfor. Without paying the slightest attention to his two sons stretched
out side by side on the ground, in the tragic attitude
of zombis, with their unseeing eyes fixed on the ceil-
ing; he sat down on the altar, and stooping over
with his head in his hands, gave himself up to the
bitterness of his plight.

Certainly he could blame no one else. It was his
fault alone. He had imprudently promised Baron
Samedi to sacrifice to him each year, a goat-without-
horns—a child—and that until the day of his death.
In return for which the Master of the Guédés, the
devilish spirits who guard the graveyards, had given
him everything his heart desired—money, love, and
great success. For the first ten years Tonton Bossa
had kept his promise, but now, either from fear or

from remorse, he felt that he had given enough and that Baron Samedi might be satisfied in other ways, but the god thought differently so he punished him cruelly through his children.

And as if this were not enough, here comes Damballa Oueddo to take part in it; and his wife, for whose sake he had done it all, turned against him publicly! That punishment surpassed all the rest in his eyes; and so poignant was his misery that life itself had no more meaning for him, and was hardly worth the pain of continuing. . . .

Yes, it was entirely his fault. In the beginning existence had not been so bad. But in those days, like his ancestors, he had regularly performed his priestly duties of houngan, in the shadow of a great ambition. Ti-Tante, his first wife, took care of the farming. She was indomitable, even though she was dried up and small of body. Untiring at work, she was even more so at love. In a word, a perfect pearl. She had given him a son who should now be in his thirties. Josaphat he was called, after an ancestor. . . . Yes, in those days his life had been no worse than that. Piously he served Damballa Oueddo and, good year or bad, his little possessions increased. Doubtless things would have rocked along the same way if Sister Cicie hadn't moved up from town, where she had worked as a servant for the bourgeois families and acquired fine manners.

He regretted nothing, however, for he snatched

everything from life that he wanted. He desired Cicie, and he had had her by paying the price. The things that followed were a result of this passion which had gripped him on the threshold of his mature age, when Cicie was still a young woman, pretty, coquettish, and sought after by all the virile men of Canapé-Vert.

In the beginning she had rejected his advances, insisting that the honest reputation of her family made it impossible for her to become his mistress. In vain he multiplied presents and promises; it did no good. Cicie, proud and inflexible, shook her head until at last Tonton Bossa, tired of the struggle, left his poor wife, Ti-Tante. But Cicie still refused, on account of his son: "Step-mothers have a bad name," she said. And this time he hardly hesitated. Not wishing to stop in the middle of the road, like Bouqui the legendary epitome of all asininity, he also broke with Josaphat. But even that didn't satisfy Cicie. She shook her head as before on the pretext that Tonton Bossa wasn't rich enough. It was then that he appealed to Baron Samedi. . . .

Meanwhile Ti-Tante had died of grief, and his son was so disgusted that he had gone to work in Cuba on the sugar plantations.

We know the rest. No! He regretted nothing, did Tonton Bossa. Besides, what good were regrets? One can never undo what has been decided by destiny.

The downpour came as a brutal interruption to the

course of his thoughts. It seemed to crush everything, patiently and continuously. It was an implacable presence that banished all others, and put
to flight the old man's sad memories. Then he
stretched himself on the ground, and closed his eyes
on the yawning emptiness of his conscience, but he
couldn't fall asleep. . . .

When the rain stopped, he opened the door and
went out. The moon shone. She had just appeared in
the eastern sky, where breaks in the clouds had left
a great watery hole, somber and chill. To the tragic
silence that follows the tempest was added the far-off
rumbling of the river in spate, and the unctuous
exhalations of the soaked earth. The trees, wet and
shining, slept like chickens with their heads under
their wings, and the breeze, coming from the bay and
neighboring isles, brought odors that were both sweet
and savage. All the countryside shivered at this cool
assault. But at times there arose from the secret
depths of the soil, in gusts, a hot breath, persuasive
and disquieting.

Suddenly, Tonton Bossa, the houngan priest, trembled. An invisible being, it seemed to him, was prowl-
ing in the yard. He thought he could hear the sound
of smothered footsteps, and a slight rustling of
starched linen. He glanced around him. Nothing. But
the "thing" came and went. Backwards and forwards.
Unable to stand it any longer, he ran to kneel at
the foot of an altar-tree consecrated to Damballa

Oueddo, and began a prayer in *langage*, the secret tongue: "Allada assou man, assou man yan, assou vil ô." . . . He couldn't go any further. Anguish choked his throat like oakum. He arose hurriedly, wet and shivering with terror. Then, without thinking, he took a path bordered by branching trees, and for a long while walked straight ahead. At times he was lost in dissembling shadows, or bathed in moonlight. Occasionally the illuminated panorama of Port-au-Prince unrolled before his eyes, but he walked rapidly, his gaze fixed and glassy, insensible to everything. His ears buzzed. He saw nothing. It passed as though the most complete night had blotted out all consciousness. He left the path and was crossing through the woods. On and on he stumbled, against rocks and the roots of big trees. . . . At last he sank down. . . .

Day had already broken when he awoke. At first his only feeling was one of pain. His cracked lips were covered with mud and blood. . . . The dawn was pale and dull. "A true awakening of a sick man," thought he. There was only the tumultuous greeting of the roosters. He looked around him with a haggard, stupefied expression, then a small glow of remembrance flickered in his mind. "But yes! That was it. . . . The little bottle. . . . Nothing but a little bottle of that liquid from the mouth of a corpse . . . And it isn't necessary to take much. . . . Only three tiny drops . . . Exactly . . . Three tiny drops. . . ."

He dragged himself painfully to his feet, and swaying from side to side, went home.

When Bobo arrived at Grande Da's to tell her the
news, the sun had been up some time. He looked to
right and left but he saw no one. Maybe they were
already in the garden. To salve his conscience, he
called softly. "Honor!"

"Respect!" came the reply from within the house.
"Who's there?"

"It's me . . . Bobo!"

Grande Da appeared at the door. "Good morning,
my son."

She seemed to be interrogating him with her eyes.
But very much upset by the scene he had just lived
through, and not knowing how to tell the news, he
didn't dare open his mouth. Disturbed by the silence
of the old woman from whom he expected some
question that might put him at his ease, and hanging
his head, he twisted his hat foolishly between his
fingers. "Grande," said he at last. "Haven't you heard
the news?"

"What news, Bobo?"

"Han!" he exclaimed, scratching his head. "I was
passing near Sister Cicie's house . . ." He became silent and looked at the old Negress covertly. She was
tragically impassive.

"I heard some shrieks in the yard . . ." He hesitated once more. What if Grande Da was to have one of her seizures! "I go in! What do I see?" He shook his head sadly. Grande Da at last showed impatience.

"But speak then, my son. Tell me what you saw."

"Sister Cicie kneeling before the corpse of Tonton Bossa. . . ."

Now that he had delivered his news he had no longer any restraint in speaking. He even gave his account with a certain volubility, not omitting the slightest detail, and described the despair of Madan Bossa. How she had taken the corpse of her husband in her arms, shaking it violently, as if to awaken it, and how at other times she had whispered tenderly in its ear. . . .

"Didn't Cicie say what had happened?" demanded Grande Da, whose voice was trembling in spite of herself.

"Oh yes! Grande, Madan Bossa talked. . . . It was this morning, she told us, that the tragedy happened. She had just opened the door when she heard a groaning in the houmfor. She hurried to see what was the matter and she fell over her husband. But by that time Tonton Bossa was stiff dead, with his eyes turned in!

"And poor Sister Cicie, how did you leave her?"

"She's no worse than that, Grande. When I left

some neighbors were making her take a little salted rum."

The old woman sighed. "But I foresaw that for Tonton Bossa. He had made promises that were too great. . . ." Then putting her hands to her mouth, she lustily hailed her family who were working at the foot of the hill.

"Hou-hou!"

"Hou-hou!"

"Prévilon ô!"

"Hou-hou!"

"Lamercie ô!"

"Hou-hou!"

"Florina ô!"

"Hou-hou!"

"Come up here, oh!"

"What is it?" asked Florina, who arrived first. But already the old woman was sobbing as custom decreed, with her head in her hands.

"Aye! . . . Aye! . . . Aye! . . . Tonton Bossa, papa, what have you done! . . . Aye! . . . Aye! . . . Florina, my child, come and help me hold my stomach so I can scream!"

The others came at last. The scene became paroxysmal. Lamercie and her daughter immediately burst into funeral lamentations, while Prévilon signified his sorrow by a series of exclamations:

"Ho! Ho! Ho! . . . Gentlemen, oh! What is this news! . . . Ho! Ho! Ho!"

The neighbors came running from all directions and in no time at all the inner yard was in a hubbub. It can be said with truth that all the chickens and the dooryard animals, and even the little house dog, took part.

CHAPTER V

"Prévilon!"

Grande Da came out of the little hut where Madan Bossa in her mourning, surrounded by all the idlers of Canapé-Vert, sobbed lugubriously. She called again, "Prévilon!"

There was no answer. Seated apart, absent-mindedly, he was evidently in one of his bad moods, a prey to the malign influence of that unknown and misleading spirit that forced him to drink and gamble.

"Prévilon!"

Still no answer. Irritated, Grande Da went over, took him by the arm and shook him roughly:

"Prévilon!"

He opened his eyes. They were like a red herring, and round.

"I'm sending you to town, do you hear?"

"Ye-es!" he replied with a yawn, stretching himself.

Grande Da shrugged her shoulders. "Here are fifty gourdes. You must buy a piece of pickled pork, three gallons of rum, five pounds of rice. . . ."

To help his memory Prévilon ticked them off on his fingers, beginning with the pork.

After she had given him his instructions, the old woman asked, "Do you understand perfectly? All right now, tell me what you're going to buy."

"Five gallons of rum, five pieces of salt pork, five pounds of rice. . . ." Poor Prévilon had already forgotten, and the old woman had to begin again. Only after the sixth time was he able to say it even halfway right.

"A piece of pickled pork, three gallons of rum, five pounds of rice. . . ." Then Grande handed him over the money.

"Prévilon," said she sternly, "I know you. Take care that your friends don't entice you to drink. Look out also when you pass near the gambling house. And also, I warn you, when you're in town, keep your eyes on the automobiles; an accident can happen so quickly."

Prévilon protested, resenting her maternal solicitude. "Maman, I'm not a child. You know that very well." He turned his back angrily and started off. Grande followed him with her eyes.

"Poor devil, Prévilon," she sighed. But he had disappeared, going at a run in spite of the heat. Naturally his throat got dry. . . .

"Hein—hein!" said he, brushing away with his hand the tempting image of three fingers of absinthe. "A promise is a promise. I shall not drink. I'm a respectable man, han!" Thus he reasoned aloud in the sincerity of his simple heart, forgetting that thirst sets a thousand traps, and that he must also watch out for his bad angel. At each bar he passed (there were four already—one might think they were multiplying that day) he had to fight temptation, and each time he triumphed heroically. It made him quite vain. His pride went to his head and flared his nostrils. But in the end his vigilance was relaxed, and when he passed Normil's bar, where he was a steady customer, the dry, sharp rattle of the dicebox reminded him that he owed the patron two gourdes. "Ho-ho!" he cried. "See what I was about to forget! Wouldn't it be better to pay him the money now when I'm thinking of it? A man should always do his duty."

"Normil," said Prévilon from the door, "I borrowed two gourdes from you. Here! I'm paying them."

Normil, apologizing to the man with whom he was

shaking dice, turned to Prévilon and took the money, feigning surprise.

"Are you sure?"

"But yes, Normil. You forget . . . The other day when I was short two gourdes. . . ."

"That's so, that's so," agreed Normil. "Now I remember."

Then winking at the man who was waiting, dice-box in hand, he said to Prévilon, looking him straight in the eye, "This is the best player in Salomon market town. But with you, he'll have to take second place."

By way of answer, the stranger looked Prévilon up and down, and with a dry, sneering voice, rolling the dice on the table, egged him on: "Seven!"

Prévilon stiffened. "Gentlemen, I'm not playing today."

"Seven!" repeated the man. He smiled disdainfully. Prévilon's pride was touched, and he felt he must accept the challenge.

"Play five gourdes!" he blurted out.

Quickly the man swept the dice into the box, shook it, and rolled "eleven" on the table. Prévilon felt hot and tired. He took off his jacket, ordered a grog which he swallowed greedily at a single gulp.

"Seven!" again said the man from Bourg-Salomon.

"Broke!" announced Prévilon firmly. An hour later he left Normil's café with bowed head. He had lost half the money his mother had given him. He was quite drunk and couldn't remember what he

was to buy in town, so there was nothing for him
to do but to go back home.

"No, no, no!" he groaned, shaking his head.
"That's too much bad luck, that! Foolish me! Here
I go to attend to serious business and, just like that, I
pass by Normil's door, and I remember I owe him
two gourdes. Bon, now, if I hadn't paid him wouldn't
that have shown a lack of consideration? But I go
in, and, without intending to, I go to gambling. . . .
No! that's too much bad luck, that! And then later,
they will tell me it's the usual thing! No, no, no!" he
tapped his foot. "Now, how much have I lost?" He
took the remaining money out of his pocket and,
shudderingly, counted it. . . . "Thirty gourdes that
I lost, gentlemen!" He was despondent and discouraged. "What can I do to make my bad spirit leave
me alone!"

One man who was quite content to have Tonton
Bossa dead was Dorvilus—Judge Dor, as everyone
called him—the chief of the rural police of the district, for that event left him the only notable of
Canapé-Vert, without competition. His tall figure,
that the years had only slightly bent, had a certain
perennial vigor. It straightened when he heard the
news at Sister Mélie's. He was returning at a gallop
from Croix-des-Missions where he had spent two

nights of dalliance with his favorite mistress—the passionate Mézine, whom, in bygone days, he had taken away from a corporal of the guard. He had gone to see Mézine each week ever since he had set his young wife up in a little business. As usual, he had stopped at Sister Mélie's, to pay a bit of court to the shopkeeper.

"Have you heard the news, judge?" asked Mélie as he was dismounting. "Tonton Bossa died this morning. And everyone says he drank the 'three drops.' "

"Don't tell me!" he answered, tying his reins to a post of the arbor. Then he explained, in an offhand manner, "I've just arrived. I've been to see my old friend, Mézine, poor devil, who's been in bed eight days with chills and fever." He lied shamelessly. But that day Sister Mélie was in no mood to tease him about his thousand and one flirtations. In a hurried breath she told him about the tragic end of Tonton Bossa. He listened to her tale without moving a muscle and appeared to be absorbed in looking at his horse. A fine beast—one must admit—but now she was all in a sweat. Her fawn coat, flecked with white, twitched at the mosquito bites, notwithstanding her tail swung from right to left, like a clock. Sometimes she stamped with her iron shoe, and this too seemed of interest to Judge Dor. At last, Sister Mélie was silent, seeking approbation with her eyes, but the only commentary was a gesture of the chief of police's hand, as if to mean, "What do you want me to say, Mélie? Life is always like that!" Then he looked at his shoes, and studied his dark-blue uniform with its shining brass buttons, and wiped his helmet with his hand. This inspection at an end, he added softly, "Bossa and I, we were friends ever since we were little children." The woman shook her head, gravely. Judge Dor arose.

"Excuse me, will you?" He cleared his throat. "I must leave you now. I'm going to see Madan Bossa."

"Ho-ho!" Sister Mélie was astonished, and felt herself in the mood for gossip. "What's hurrying you like that?"

"I've got to go home first, to change my clothes."

The shopkeeper smiled with malice. "How could you look any better? If you could only see how fine you are!"

And the judge who was vulnerable to praise, like most of the people in the world, thanked her by a sound slap on her buttocks that were firm and well-rounded.

"Ah! that Sis Mélie!" said he, seeing she was slightly agitated and laughing dryly. Then he jumped into his saddle, spurred his horse, and left at a gallop as he had come. . . .

Mélie had well said that Judge Dor was a fine figure of a man! He had charm and was a real leader of men—as well as of women! Alas! It was much against his wishes that Mélie had not succumbed to his advances. She wasn't hard to please nor was she coquettish but there was a rumor current about Dorvilus that was not reassuring. It was said, whether right or wrong, that he had murdered his son, Actéon, the only child he had had by Sister Tia, his principal wife. It was a tale disquieting enough in other respects. . . . But the main fact was that the boy had taken in his mother when she left the judge's roof because he used to beat her severely on his bad days. Dorvilus had reasoned to himself this way: "If that son of mine, the little Negro, didn't give her food and drink, could you believe that that woman would have trifled with me that way?" In consequence he had poisoned his boy, and as he had foreseen, his wife returned to him right after the funeral. That's what they said. To be sure, Mélie did not attach much importance to the tale, which might be only gossip, but when there is any doubt it is wise to be careful, so she religiously defended her virtue, difficult as that was to do.

The yard was full of people when Judge Dor arrived at Madan Bossa's house. They had come partly to help the widow, partly to gloat over the defunct. Forewarned by a friend, Grande came out, solemnly, to greet the chief of police who immediately made excuses for his tardiness. "I only just arrived. I've been over to Croix-des-Missions about a matter of land."

"A matter of land! He had nerve to say that!" Grande Da smiled with a knowing air.

"So it's this way that Bossa left us," he said hypocritically, flattered deeply that she had guessed the truth. "Me, I would have believed he had more courage in misfortune. The last time we saw each other, after the disappearance of Exanthus, he seemed broken up. That's true, but I didn't think it was to this point!"

Grande Da gave a conventional sigh. Then, taking him familiarly by the hand, she bade him enter the house.

"Judge, come see Sister Cicie. . . ."

Madan Bossa was lying on her pallet, silently, with unseeing eyes. Her face, which was usually a rich black, had under the blows of sorrow taken on a slightly rusty tinge like bodies exposed in the morgue. Florina and Lamercie were wailing in turns, holding their stomachs carefully. At times, when they could do no more, some charitable neighbor relayed them.

Judge Dor paid his respects to Madan Bossa, and in spite of the hubbub of the mourners, she heard him. Coming out of her prostration, she looked at him brokenheartedly. It was her only thanks!

He was moved. In other days hadn't he loved her too? She had tormented him like the itch, as she had all the rest of the men in the neighborhood . . . She had certainly preferred the dead man to him. But in the presence of sorrow, no one can boast of being resentful. He turned his helmet between his fingers, overcome with emotion. The time was interminable. . . . At last, according to custom, Grande took him to see the corpse.

While they were making their way to the houmfor, where they had placed the body of Tonton Bossa, the old woman gave a start; poor Prévilon was returning from his errand with empty hands!

"It isn't my fault! I kept the money in my pants pocket like this. And then when I got to town, the idea popped into my head that I should count it. I pulled out the money. I look at it. I count; ho-ho! Thirty gourdes are missing. Maman, may the good Lord send the lightning to break me in two, if it wasn't the Haoussas—those thieving spirits—who took the money."

Grande Da knew very well what had gone on; besides it wasn't necessary to guess, for Prévilon's breath proved he had been drinking, and, if he had been drinking, it was certain he had gambled. Were not these two vices always associated, hand in hand?

"What business have you to talk like that, Prévilon?" said Grande Da angrily. "I've already seen what's the matter; you have smoked and gambled and drunk away the thirty gourdes!"

"Maman, I ask the good Lord. . . ."

"Listen, Prévilon, don't try to treat me like a child. Give me the rest of my money!"

"May the Virgin blast my two eyes, if it wasn't the Haoussas. . . ."

"Give me the rest of my money!" repeated Grande, as inflexible as Destiny, holding out her hand.

Prévilon was beside himself. He felt humiliated. He had entirely forgotten he was lying, and he felt that the public dishonor his mother was inflicting upon him was an injustice, so he called on everybody as witness, "Oh, my friends, have you ever met a human being who traveled in such hard luck as I? A son whose mother vilifies him so undeservedly?" But the real climax came when the old woman told Aladin, the lover of his daughter, to make the purchases in his place. "That's pretty hard!" he remarked, profoundly disheartened. "To do that to me, to me, the respectable father of a family! But that's what they say: 'If you render a service, you reap only sorrow.'" He tried to fit a moral to his tale, but it was Judge Dor (as was proper) who achieved that honor, for as Grande was leading him to the houmfor, he said in a tone that could be heard by all, "My old friend, do you know that in this matter you must punish the man, but pardon the alcohol. . . ."

The entrance to the shrine was hung with leafy branches of orange trees and thorny acacia, so that the soul of the dead would not be tempted to leave.

Inside, on the adobe walls, pictures of the saints done in the crudest, Saint-Sulpice manner, were tacked up. They represented the loas, or spirits of the Vodun pantheon. Sacred stones, some of them pre-Columbian, were on the altar, the little burnt-clay pots containing the souls of the initiates, and all the other ceremonial objects—the crucifix, the gourd rattle or tchatchas, the bells, the bottle of liquor, and the big enameled goblets used for making libations. The Arada drums hung from the roofbeams by iron wires.

Covered by a sheet, the corpse of the houngan, Bossa, was laid on the door of the houmfor which had been removed for the occasion and propped up on boxes at either end. Grande Da uncovered the face. It was terrifying. The eyelids were only half shut; a bandage of linen kept his jaw from falling open, and his lips, twisted by a cynical grin, drew back over revolting teeth that looked like white worms. But over his face was the solemnity of the dead, at once tragic and ridiculous.

A smile of triumph flitted furtively across Dorvilus' face, but having respect for the conventions, he crossed himself.

CHAPTER VI

THE celebrated houngan of Bizoton, the infallible Boispirhaut, had been sent for to conduct Tonton Bossa's funeral in accordance with Ouan-Zen rites. He was an impressive being, with a phantasmal, legendary appearance. As tall as a bamboo pole, he had a bent back, an angular bony face, dull eyes, and a nasal drawling basso that was painful to hear. In short, he looked like a guédé, or spirit, on a visit from the other world. He had come to Bizoton about twenty years before, and no one knew where he came from. Ever since, he had performed prodigies. Trustworthy witnesses insisted that they had seen him, on certain nights, hovering silently in the sky like a bird of prey; others that he possessed the miraculous power of changing the land of Haiti into a desert or, at will, making it a paradise of abundance. That he had done nothing at all was merely evidence of his great benevolence.

It was generally believed that he came to that part of the country by a master stroke, for competing with an ancient houngan, with whose work in magic he seemed to be eternally interfering, he had incurred the old man's anger. Feeling compelled to challenge Boispirhaut to a duel in order to retain his prestige, and influence with his patrons, he sent the summons.

They met at midnight in a lonely neighborhood, near a cemetery. Being younger and braver, Boispirhaut was the first to attack, so he seized his adversary by the collar; but the older man had acquired more than one "power" in the course of his career and was able to transform himself into a snake, and slipped through his adversary's hands. Seeing this Boispirhaut changed himself into a cat, and to foil this unexpected maneuver, the old houngan took the form of a grain of corn, but with blasting adroitness Boispirhaut changed himself into a cock and swallowed his rival. . . .

This is how Boispirhaut's reputation was established in Haiti and even beyond the frontiers of the republic, for the story spread from one end of the island to the other, and it was not a rare occurrence, according to common report, for the "servants" of the eastern end to call on his great knowledge.

Since then, he had adopted as a uniform a blue pajama top embroidered with gold threads, and black spy glasses. And when he was called in consultation he took with him a mysterious valise just like the doctors carry. . . . It was in this amazing costume that he approached Tonton Bossa's corpse that evening, already surrounded by a dozen or more squatting hounsis.

He drew back for an instant, just enough time to murmur a prayer, shook his head, and directed his steps toward the altar. Quickly seizing the gourd rattle, or açon, he gave it three dry, short shakes in a solemn manner; to the right for the Arada spirits, in the center for the Pétro, to the left for the Congo. Then, without anyone knowing just why (but possibly this was characteristic showmanship) he vigorously intoned one of those songs called "chante-point" that did not belong in the Vodun ritual:

> "Cà ou ouè, çà ou ouè là-là,
> Cà m'dit, çà m'dit là-là,
> Cà ou ouè, pin'ga palé,
> Cà ou tendé, pin'ga palé!
> Ou cé ti-moune ca grands-mounes.
> Cà ou ouè là-à,
> Cou ou palé, ou a chaudé!"

It was a warning that if his listeners revealed the mystic wonders they were about to hear and see, they would certainly burn for it.

And Judge Dor, who combined the duties of an
officer of the rural police with the lucrative business
of being a houngan, thought that he in his turn
should improvise on the same theme:

> "Ya coulé, oh! ya coulé!
> Ya coulé, oh! ya coulé!
> Cé Messiés-à-yo qui ouè çà nous pé fait.
> Yo dit yap' fait-li tou!
> Ya coulé, oh! ya coulé!
> Ya coulé, oh! ya coulé!"

This was another warning as to what would happen
to those who were not tight-lipped or might boast of
being able to duplicate the houngan's accomplish-
ments.

Then Boispirhaut, not to be outdone, sang:

> "Lan perron-moin, m' cé grand-moune.
> Lan houmfor-moin, m' cé grand-moune.
> Ca qui couè m'mentô,
> Ya vini la-caille-moin!"

> "On my doorstep, I am all powerful.
> In my temple, I am all powerful.
> Anyone who thinks I lie
> Has only to come to my house."

It was after this menacing, fantastic prelude that
Boispirhaut began the ceremony. He pinched up flour

between his thumb and forefinger from a faïence bowl ornamented with red and blue flowers, and drew on the ground a cabalistic design of a snake and other esoteric figures symbolizing Damballa Oueddo. Then, at his invitation, Grande Da and Judge Dor came in turn to complete the magic pattern whose stylization was reminiscent of tapestry, and the rhythmic deformations of primitive Negro sculpture. The hieroglyphs were then watered by the initiates who, according to his rank, took turns in kissing certain of the designs. This rite performed, they proceeded from Boispirhaut to Grande Da, not omitting Judge Dor, to genuflect and give the password. This was done to the continuous handclapping accompaniment of the whole assembly who joined in singing:

"Damballah Oueddo
Dan qui si sala do,
Do qui do, silibobo
Ayibobo!"

Three low chairs were then brought in for the principal dignitaries, and while the hounsis, as if obsessed, danced around the body of Tonton Bossa, Boispirhaut recited in a tremulous voice litanies in Latin, in Creole, and in *langage,* and strangely mingled in them were the names of loas with their African sounds, and the saints of the Roman Catholic

Calendar. The company made responses in a low voice as at early mass, at four o'clock in the morning. This took a long time. The hounsis turned and turned and turned; and Boispirhaut bleated. No one but received a tribute, even to the Mother of Christ:

"Gracia Sancta Maria!
Gracia Sancta Maria, maraine, oh!
Gracia Sancta Maria!
Gracia Sancta Maria, maraine, oh!
Moin dit grâce, m'apé mandé padon!
Moin dit grâce, m'apé mandé padon!
Lapriè pou la Sainte Viège Marie!
Moin dit grâce, m'apé mandé padon!
Lapriè pou la Sainte Viège Marie!
Moin dit grâce m'apé mandé padon!
Maraine, oh! Paraine, oh! Domine!"

The "Our Father" and "Hail Mary" were also recited with the same fervor as in the Roman Catholic Church. Then the door of the houmfor was shut in the faces of the guests, who scattered around the yard where drinks, spareribs, and other appetizing viands were being served under arbors erected for the occasion. Boispirhaut extinguished the two crude lamps with floating wicks that lit the sanctuary with a dirty yellow light, and kneeling near the corpse, he addressed it for a long time in a low voice. Then he broke into song again:

"Hèritiers n'âme yo, côté nous yé?
Héritiers n'âme yo, côtè nous yé?
Si m' té gagnin bon fami,
Si m' té gagnin bons pitites,
Yo ta lévé lan dômi vin' chéri loa-yo!"

"Inheritors of the soul, where are you?
Inheritors of the soul, where are you?
If I had a good family,
If I had good children,
They will awake to cherish their loa."

At length, shaking the bell and the gourd rattle, he called the dead man, insistently: "Tonton Bossa! . . . Tonton Bossa! . . . Tonton Bossa, Bossa! . . ." The women of the family flung themselves on the corpse and screamed as if in the pains of childbirth. But deaf to their appeal, Tonton Bossa, who should have opened his eyes, sat up in his coffin, and talked like a living human being, clung shamelessly to his macabre immobility, and even seemed to enjoy it. All the while the hounsis circled around him, circled and circled and circled. Boispirhaut began again in his sepulchral voice: "Tonton Bossa. . . . Tonton Bossa, don't you understand that your whole family is here calling for you!" But the trouble was to no avail! And the bell and rattle proved themselves powerless. The dead man was tied up in his own thoughts; it was plain to see and no one doubted it.

But the houngan persisted, and made it a matter of personal pride: "Tonton Bossa. . . . All your relatives are here, yes! . . . They are asking for you . . . Tonton Bossa, rise up to speak to them! . . . Tonton Bossa! . . ." He didn't move. Then a light was made and at a sign from Boispirhaut the people retired to a near-by room, leaving him alone with the corpse.

What happened in their absence, no one ever knew. But the fact remains that they were convinced that the expected miracle took place. However, when they returned to the sanctuary at the call of Boispirhaut, the houngan triumphantly held in his hand a burnt-clay jar in which he had gathered, so it was supposed, the soul of Tonton Bossa, plucked from his remains. He placed the pot in the new houmfor which had been recently built by Tonton Bossa, and which that day a prêtre savane, or bush priest, had come to consecrate. It would not be open until a year and a day after the ceremony, and then the spirits could choose a live successor to the corpse and indicate their selection by "possessing" him.

A procession was formed and Ti-Dan marched at the head, carrying a saber to show that he was master of ceremonies. He bounded around like an angry beast and twirled his weapon in dangerous circles to scare away any evil spirits. Two hounsi standard-bearers followed him, then a group of canzos or neophytes, the choir of bossals, the servants of the houn-

gan, Grande Da, Judge Dor, and Boispirhaut carrying the precious pot. The relatives and guests, who
had abandoned their cards, dice and dominoes, joined
the procession and marched on the mattings that had
been laid like a path. It was a plaintive, touching
elegy that they sang with all the power and dignity
of a "De Profundis." It sounded the theme of the
persistent nostalgia for the precious earth of Africa
that has always affected the peasants of Haiti:

> "Loa Zao, qui côté nous yé?
> Lao Zao ô-ô, lan Guinin nous sôti!
> Là n' té yé!
> Loa Zao, qui côté nous yé?
> Loa Zao ô-ô, lan Guinin nous sôti!
> Là n' té yé!
> O bel, oh! qui misè, qui la-peine, qui tracas,
> Qui metté nous, là, oh!"

Sorrowfully they questioned the loa Zao and asked
why had they come from Guinea? What misery, what
pain, what trouble had put them here!

When the shrine was reached Grande Da solemnly
gave the keys to Boispirhaut, who opened the door,
approached the altar, and placed the sacred jar before
a large image of the Trinity which was feebly lighted
by eternal lamps. Then kneeling he kissed the earth,
and everything that had happened in the beginning

of the evening was repeated: cabalistic designs, libations, invocations, litanies, etc. . . .

At last to conclude the service Grande Da and Boispirhaut danced grotesquely in honor of Papa Nibo, with the hounsis circling around them to tunes of a carabineer's song. This was in accordance with the ritual providing that all ceremonies shall conclude with an homage to the spirits of hell:

> "Papa Guédé bel gaçon,
> Guédé Nibo bel gaçon!
> L'habillé-l' tout en blanc,
> Pou l'al' monté au Palais!
> Lors l'habillé-l' tout en jaune,
> Li pôtrait gnou sénatè!

> "Papa Guédé bel gaçon,
> Guédé Nibo bel gaçon!
> L'habillé-l' tout en blanc,
> Pou l'al' monté au Palais!
> Lors l'habillé-l' tout en noi,
> Li pôtrait gnou dépité.
> Lors l'habillé-l' tout en blanc,
> Li pôtrait gnou jasmin double."

It ended in fulsome praise of the god, saying that when he was dressed in white he looked like a double jasmine.

The dance broke up in general abandon, the houn-

sis staggering around and making the raucous sounds
of those "possessed"—a real debauch!

While the crowd of guests were scattering around
the yard, eager for the diversions usual at wakes,
Boispirhaut drew Grande Da aside. He took her hands
and in a sepulchral voice talked to her of the curse
her family would call down on Canapé-Vert if she
did not circumvent Tonton Bossa's heritage of harm.
Everything must be sold—the houses, the lime kilns,
and even the land. He evidently realized what a
painful sacrifice this would be, especially in the matter of the property. But there was no other method
of appeasing the wrath of Baron Samedi. . . . Unless . . . but who would be temerarious enough to
be willing to keep the dead man's terrible promises?

Grande Da knew that Boispirhaut's advice was
wise, and she agreed to follow all his suggestions to
the letter. Finally Boispirhaut said, in his most distant and detached manner, that in those circumstances he would undertake, for the moderate price
of one thousand gourdes, to restore their souls to the
two zombis, Philoxène and Exanthus.

With every possible and imaginable precaution,
Grande Da insinuated by indirection that this sum
was far beyond Madan Bossa's means. Boispirhaut
brusquely let go her hand and, drawing himself up
to his full height, showed that he was much offended.
So Grande Da, to placate him, agreed to his price;
then Boispirhaut unbent. He explained heatedly and

with great luxury of detail, that the Baron was a most
exigent personage and that a long series of ceremonies
and sacrifices were necessary to bring him around. To
tell the truth, the thousand gourdes, which he asked,
was only a price between friends, and hardly enough
to pay expenses. . . .

From the house where Madan Bossa lay unconscious, came the clamor of noisy hymns, boisterously
bawled in a silly languishing manner. The wake was
in full spate. The moon disappeared behind a great
black cloud outlined in silver, that floated slowly
from the sea on the wings of the west wind. Seated
near the fires eating, men and women roared with
laughter at stories most of which had already de-
lighted many generations—stories that had lost no
savor by constant retelling, for each reciter revivified
them with his own wit. Other guests, their faces
glistening with sweat, their eyes red, their breath
fetid, vociferated loudly as they struck the tables
with dice cups or dominoes. Others, more reserved,
indulged in interminable card games. The wind,
searching through the whole countryside, blew under
the large kettles, raising and lowering the flames,
lighting up the somber faces, or blotting them out
altogether. . . . The serving was done by young girls
dressed in white, who passed quickly from one group
to another, carrying large trays loaded with cups of
coffee or infusions of the leaves of the malagueta—
pepper tree. Sometimes they had a glass and bottle

and served the thirsty males two or three fingers
of rum. And as they passed a swarm of flattering
compliments followed them while their brown lips
opened in smiles on the white teeth of virtue and
innocence. But under cover of the general uproar,
pairs of lovers escaped into the warm, languorous
night. Many new matings were decided upon that
evening, and upon a couch of grass or even the bare
earth, dramas and delights were elicited in wild, violent embraces.

Boispirhaut and Judge Dor did not mix with the
crowd, their age and dignity kept them apart from
the noise of it all. After discussing supernatural ill-
nesses, poisonous leaves and roots, they came inevitably to the case of Tonton Bossa. As to Boispirhaut,
the matter was not at all clear to him, but there must
have been some vengeance involved. And this he said,
looking with suspicion at the chief of police who,
with a furtive expression, insisted upon recalling the
evil promises of the defunct. . . .

Aladin passed close by without seeing them. He
had arrived after the ceremony and was worried
about Florina, whom he had not yet seen. He brought
with him a young man of exotic appearance, dressed
in a sea-blue coat, flannel trousers, black-and-white
shoes, a large, gray felt sombrero, à la Mexicaine, and
further adorned with huge tortoise-shell spectacles.
In a word, a caballero. This important-looking personage talked with an exuberance and emphasis truly

Castilian, and with a self-satisfaction seasoned his conversation plentifully with curse words and Spanish expressions. He often took off his impressive glasses, wiped them on his sleeve and replaced them on his nose.

At last Aladin saw Florina. Without taking the trouble to excuse himself to his companion, he immediately rushed over to the young girl.

"Oh, Florina!" said he, taking her gently by the arm, "where have you been? Ever since I got here I've been looking for you."

"It's not my fault, Aladin. But today you know I don't belong to myself."

"I'm not reproaching you, but when you are not there nothing seems right to me. Look! Tonight I haven't even had a small drink!"

This seemed to bother Florina and she placed her hand affectionately on the young man's shoulder. "You're in earnest, Aladin," she said. "You haven't yet been served! Well, then you can sit down. I'm going to bring you something."

Aladin held her back and pointed out his friend who was looking at them with a calculating eye. "Don't you know him, Florina?"

"Hein—hein!" she said, shaking her head. "Who is it?"

"It's Josaphat, yes. . . . Don't you remember him? . . . The son of Tonton Bossa and Ti-Tante. The one who went to Cuba. . . . He returned this afternoon, and since he is my baptismal brother he came to my house. . . ."

"What a fine-looking boy," exclaimed Florina enthusiastically.

Aladin looked gloomy. His face hardened with pain, his lips took on an ill-natured expression. But Florina didn't notice it. She smiled at Josaphat and appeared fascinated. . . . Thoughtfully Aladin rejoined his companion.

"What a girl! Who's that you were speaking with, Aladin?"

"It's Florina," Aladin replied dryly. "The daughter of Prévilon and Lamercie."

"Cogno!" exploded Josaphat, his eyes shining with eager desire. "I've seen some good-looking ones in Cuba, but nunca, never like that young girl."

Aladin made an effort to control himself. He did not wish to appear rude. "José!" said he. (Josaphat, like all those who return from Cuba or Santo Domingo, had Hispanicized his name.) "José! You see, Florina, I couldn't tell you, and you couldn't understand how much I love her. You remember when you went away, she was still at the creeping stage. . . . Well! I, myself, have remained here, watched her grow up, watched her develop into that beautiful Negress you have just seen. . . . She's for me! Not longer ago than March I asked her family for her. That we haven't already set up housekeeping is because my crops didn't sell very well this year. . . ."

Florina interrupted his confession. She stood before them smiling, a glass in one hand and a bottle in the other. "Here's what I've brought you," she said.

José fondled her with his eyes, touching her hips, her breasts, lightly glancing over her soft black skin that was so cool, Bon Dieu! that one would think she had drenched it in the night for hours. Her eyes wavered at his glances, so subtle and all-inclusive. But a violent, apprehensive fear mingled with her pleasure and darkened its luster; she remembered the predictions of Grande Erzilie and of the young man she had seen in a dream sinking with her in dirty water. She didn't recall his face, and still for all that, she was sure that José looked like him. . . .

"I've just told my brother that I've seen beautiful women in Cuba, but nunca like you," José said.

Her only reply to the compliment was a sad little smile. Aladin wanted to pick José up in his big hands and break him apart like a clod of earth. But Florina turned her head, and making excuses in a trembling voice, went away. . . .

Nevertheless, the alcohol soon mollified Aladin's heart, diffusing a pleasant warmth in his veins. He even reproached himself for his sudden fit of jealousy that he concluded was without foundation, for he was tender and good-humored by nature. José told him about Cuba, the fine things he had seen, the good and the bad days he had lived through. He let himself be soothed by the singsong exotic accent of

José, not even trying to visualize the wonders he described. Afterward they talked of their childhood in Canapé-Vert. All rivalry had disappeared—their friendship was re-established. . . .

"Aladin!" suddenly croaked a voice hoarse with rum. The two friends started. Near them, the intruder was keeping his feet with difficulty. His shirttail fluttering in the breeze, slapped his buttocks grotesquely. "Say! One doesn't come to a wake to sit on one's behind, as you're doing. That's no good. Come, get up. It's almost dawn; it's time for the forfeit games." Perceiving José, he added with a hostile air, "Possibly you would prefer to stay where you are!"

"Oh no!" protested José, smiling. "I want to play, and I'm ready, too."

Already the enthusiasts of three-seven were pocketing their cards, and the dominoes had been put away in their boxes for a long time. But the sharp clicking sound of the dice cups could still be heard.

According to custom, the games that closed the wake began. First came rather infantile verses in Creolized French, mean and insupportably silly: "Trois fois, passez-là, c'est la de' nié' qui 'estera . . . Les z'ongnons, les z'ongnons qui 'taient bon ma'ché . . . Nous sommes trois frè' qui voulons nous marier . . . Au bo' dé l'eau, in bal fit annoncé . . . etc. . . ." Then a couple would act out an amorous

pursuit with a great deal of grace—a young girl
escaping from an overeager gallant through the
crowd that sang with clapping hands:

"Oui, cé li même!
Oui, cé li même!
Viège Tiotiote, cé li même!
Aye! maman-m', cé li même!"

Chairs were brought, placed in a circle, and Aladin
took the center. He pulled a silk handkerchief out of
his pocket, called three of his friends, and said, "Let
each of you take a corner. When I say 'pull,' you let
go. When I say 'let go,' you pull. Good; ready! Then
he passed his hand over the handkerchief, made believe he was composing some verses, all the while
dancing with his shoulders and singing:

"N'a mangé ti pains chauds,
Ti pains chauds ca Madan Beaupin,
Ah! ti pains chauds ca Madan Beaupin,
Ti pains chauds ca Madan Beaupin,
Cé ti pains chauds ca, ti pains chauds,
Ti pains chauds ca Madan Beaupin!"

It was a childlike song that repeated, over and
over again, that they were going to eat some of Madame Beaupin's little hot biscuits.

Aladin made a sign to one of the spectators, and

said, "Hold it for me." He approached a young girl
and put his hand on her head. It was part of the
game for her to take offense and repulse him roughly,
saying, "Dirty nigger, go wash your feet."

At that moment Aladin gave a cry of surprise. He
had just seen José and Florina, seated side by side, in
a tender tête-à-tête. He staggered, put his hand on
his heart, and painfully dragged himself toward them,
without paying the least attention to the remon-
strances of his companions. One might have said his
feet were gripped in sticky mud.

"José!" he called feebly. His eyes haggard, he
straightened up before them. His lips trembled convulsively. "José, we'll go down to the house."

José followed him with poor grace; but he could
do nothing else, having taken lodging with Aladin;
besides, it was beginning to rain, and people were
leaving hurriedly.

CHAPTER VII

The tops of the trees bent under the weight of the wind then straightened again, cracking and groaning. A cold rain spilled itself in tiny drops, and sometimes the chilly plaint of a bird was heard melting into the penetrating sadness and humidity. As they traveled briskly in the darkness, Aladin slipped and fell. José, who followed him, ran up and took him by the arm to help him up; he was weighted with suffering, his head hung on his chest.

"You didn't hurt yourself, chico?" asked José.

Aladin regarded him with a wandering look, shook his head and murmured as if out of himself, "I'd kill her first." José shivered, realizing he spoke of Florina,

but he didn't dare say a word. Besides, what could
he do in the circumstances, if by the will of the
spirits matters came to that?

Aladin went on in a hard, decisive voice: "In my
family, José, we have a very small heart. It has no
room for trespass or treason." He got to his feet
and started off again.

When they reached home it was José who lit the
lamp for, without taking the trouble to undress,
Aladin had thrown himself on his mat as if from the
top of a mountain. To sink! To drown himself and
his sorrow in death—ah! What a deliverance that
would be . . . Two large tears beaded his cheeks,
and he turned over on his face, ashamed of his weakness. Suffering filled him to the brim. It was there,
inescapable, like the pain in his stomach that had
overtaken him the previous year when, having voted
at the election, he drank too ardently and ate too
much. Sanite had relieved him with heated bricks.
And now she wasn't here any more to take care of
him with the greatness of heart of the homely woman
. . . so homely that her devotion had become odious. . . . When he had driven her away, Sanite herself had said to him, "Beautiful woman, great misfortune." And certainly she had spoken the truth,
that unlucky wench!

Little by little consciousness vanished. Sleep
mounted in him like the cold of agony. Florina's
face gradually melted away, one feature after an-

other. Then everything disappeared. But if the pain
had deserted his soul, it still flayed his flesh, secretly
and as far as the obscure recesses of his instinct.

José too had gone to bed, his hands under his head.
He looked out through the door he had left open,
so much did he mistrust his companion. From time
to time he secretly watched Aladin, when his matting cracked under the sudden jerkings of his an-
guished body.

At last, not able to abide it any longer, he called
Aladin and asked him how he felt. He got no answer.
His anxiety grew. It seemed to him that Aladin's
sleep was merely a pretense. A terrifying vision captured his overexcited imagination—a vision of Aladin, his face disfigured by rage, hacking a body with
a machete. He jumped to his feet with the cry of a
wounded man, and stood for an instant paralyzed
with fright. Aladin never stirred. Maybe he was really
asleep; but how could one be sure? "Aladin," called
José in a low voice. "Aladin, don't you hear me,
chico?" Aladin didn't answer. He didn't dare go near
him. Indeed it was an intolerable anguish. And the
night complained so lugubriously outside! José took
a chair and went to sit under the arbor facing the
door, ready to flee at the least noise.

Here too, other torments awaited him. Florina.
. . . It was certainly not for his happiness that he
had met her. On the eve of his departure from San-
tiago, didn't his poor mother come to him in a dream

to adjure him to never again set foot on the accursed ground of Canapé-Vert? But a strange power, more obstinate than love, had forced him to return, and it was neither homesickness nor that puissant bond that rivets the country Negro to the land of his ancestors. He had returned, without doubt led by fate, and the drama had immediately begun. "I'll kill her first," Aladin had declared. And he would surely do it. José never doubted it. But how to avoid the misfortune? Fate had already bound him to Florina, he felt it, and his will power could do nothing against it, for to fight against the loas is impossible. Aladin's words haunted him implacably, eating into him like a worm, and at each thrust of pain he shuddered. Ah yes, his dead father, the old he-goat, had made a mess! And all that for the damned old sorceress of a Sor Cicie who had bewitched him!

It was his turn now to be tested. But no menace would separate him from Florina. She was his forever, in life as in death; and Aladin could say what he liked, for it was a chain as strong as the will of God, forged by Destiny. Yet he had never spoken to her of love. Only the usual talk between strangers who meet somewhere on earth. But a secret sweetness had flowed from one to the other that was more imperious than fear or joy . . . From that time on he had known and had taken his decision. Madan Bossa, relinquishing her claim to the inheritance from Ton-ton Bossa, as was right in such a case, he would receive it for himself alone, with the love and the curse; Baron Samedi doubtless wished it that way. . . .

Dawn came so gently that the roosters hardly realized it. The first one to be heard was Ti-Dan's—a hoarse old warrior with only one eye. Prévilon's fighters replied to him immediately, Aladin's, and Bobo's, and Zinzin's. And soon at Musseau, Bourdon, Gros-Morne, Moronvil, and Source-Turgeau a great clamor arose that spread like fire in a canefield; the cocks coming to life from place to place, one after another.

The evening star paled on the horizon, white as a coffee blossom. Already the deafening noise of the pestle could be heard coming from Sor Mélie's yard. It was the time of day to wash both mouth and eyes. José entered the dwelling looking for water. Filling a glass he made it ring against the pitcher; Aladin was curled up in the same place . . . still he did not move.

After the last prayers were said Prévilon had hastily built a small shack in Grande Da's yard to lodge, for better or for worse, Madan Bossa and her two zombis. She had left her own house without showing the slightest regret. Since the death of her man she had been slightly out of her head and mumbled to herself all day long.

Hardly had she abandoned her house before José

moved in. They had tried to dissuade him, but he had shaken his head with a sullen, resigned air, saying he had no other means of support except to farm his father's property. Naturally this had not brought him any luck. Not only had the houngan's cash, of which he had expected to receive his share, disappeared as if by enchantment (following custom, perhaps Tonton Bossa had hidden it somewhere in the garden), but also José himself had soon become the pet aversion of Canapé-Vert, everyone unanimously predicting that he would bring down curses upon the entire region. No one wanted to work on his land, the lime kilns had no hands to fire them, so that to keep from poverty he was forced to toil all alone, and in a small way, within the limits of his own strength. Likewise Sor Mélie, so agreeable to everybody, kept him at a distance like a pest. But José worried only about Florina. "What difference does all the rest make?" he said, and took this for truth.

In the days that followed Tonton Bossa's wake she had become his mistress after a sharp "explanation" with Aladin, who had threatened to kill her. Each evening at nightfall José met her in the bushes near the spring of Jecrois. Then they embraced in a gloomy and despairing intoxication. When she discovered it, Grande Da's blood curdled, as was right. Seizing a big stick she had beaten Florina, who owed her life that night to the intervention of the neighbors. Since that time, the old woman had never ceased to visit all kinds of misery on her. But the worst was that Florina was convinced she was ruining herself, as well as her family and all the inhabitants of Canapé-Vert. This did not prevent her, nevertheless, from going out each night to meet José.

Already everything was turning against her. By way of vengeance Aladin circulated the most disagreeable stories about her, which people hurried to spread everywhere. He never let an occasion go by to soil her reputation, especially when he was asked if she had really been his woman, as rumor had it, and if she was ardent in love and good-natured. Without saying so outright, he shrugged his shoulders and laughed at the right time.

In addition to which Florina now had other discomforts. Her head swam sometimes and she had uncontrollable fits of vomiting. José urged her to live with him; but even though she knew this was an unavoidable reckoning, she forced herself to delay it as long as possible, hoping perhaps that meanwhile something would happen to change the course of her life. . . .

One morning, going to the spring by a roundabout way, she ran into Aladin at a turn in the road. Their meeting could not have been more dangerous, for on each side of the path grew the high stalks of a

planting of millet in full splendor. Florina gave a
long stifled cry when he seized her. All of a sudden
her strength left her, and he was able to throw her
on the ground without any effort. Her eyes grew
big with terror when she saw above her an unrecog-
nizable face, hard and avid, twisted by hate and
desire. But as his hands adventured beneath her dress,
she squeezed her thighs together and tried to push him
away.

It was a savage struggle and merciless! He struck
her in the face with the flat of his hand, seeking to
stun her while she tried to scratch his eyes out. He
struck slowly, with regular blows, blow after blow.
. . . At last she cried, "Help! . . . Assassin! . . ."
He placed his hand over her mouth. It was just what
she wanted so that she could bite him to the quick.
She did it with a cruel pleasure.

In vain he tried to make her let go her hold;
Florina's teeth tore him terribly. Then he pulled with
the frenzied energy of an animal caught in a trap,
and suddenly fell backward. . . . Without losing
any time, Florina picked up her calabash and fled
headlong.

She rushed home and threw herself at her grandmother's feet. Showing her bruised face, her dress
soiled and torn, she sobbed, "It's Aladin, yes, who did
this to me!"

Without saying anything, his face impressed with
a majestic anger, Prévilon armed himself with a stick

and his machete. Grande Da looked at him with astonishment.

"Where are you going, my son?" she demanded.

"No!" he answered. "You have no son at this moment. It's on my return that you will know if you still have a son."

Lamercie ran to the door to bar his passage, while Grande Da, clinging to him, tried to make him listen to reason.

"Let me go, maman! Let me go now!" He made such a row that in the end the old woman obeyed him. Prévilon didn't expect that, no! He was completely disarmed. It must be realized that he was of gentle character and his only excesses were gambling and drink.

"That's not right what Aladin did," at last said Grande Da to her granddaughter. "But realize, also, if you were not having an affair with José, all this would never have happened."

Thus Florina was forced to swallow her tears and her shame.

CHAPTER VIII

TWILIGHT lingered. The
agony of the sun had abated to a gentle glow that
still lighted the sky, the houses and the tender pay-
sage of the hills. It was an evil augury, and the people of Canapé-Vert had only too many reasons for
alarm. Even the hearts that were already bowed by
the most dreadful anxieties were affrighted anew that
night. For Carmen, the wife of Zinzin, a blind impatience mingled with her anguish. She was not to
be resigned, no, and couldn't see why Tonton Bossa's
misfortune, through José's fault, should descend on
her and hers. But as she could accomplish nothing
by her own efforts, she directed her bad humor at the
fire logs and the cooking utensils, which she threw
around angrily while preparing the evening meal.

Orphise, the older of the two children she had with Zinzin, played in the yard with her little brother, whom she was supposed to take care of, as custom decreed. Their innocent nudity had for its sole protection a covering of dust and dirt; their stomachs were swollen by intestinal worms, their navels protruded, and their noses were besmirched; but that couldn't keep them from living, growing and amusing themselves, for that is the usual condition of little Negroes in the country, and there was no reason why they should be different from the others. All day they had indulged in their pastimes. Now they rested, lying on the very ground from which they seemed to have sprung—having the same color. They had already exhausted their repertory of songs and while waiting the turn of the stories and riddles that only come at night, Orphise pretended to be asleep, but her brother, the insatiable Anacius, dragged her from her drowsiness.

"Sheep!" said he.

"Baa!" replied Orphise, rubbing her eyes.

"Where are you going?"

"I'm going to the slaughterhouse."

"When will you come back?"

"Never, never, never, never!"

It was just then that Bonaccueil, Zinzin's cousin, came along. He was returning to Carrefour-Laboule from town where he had gone to see one of his daughters he had placed in a bourgeois family.

"Good evening, cousin!" said he, with his hat in his hand, having stopped politely at the entrance to the yard.

"Ho-ho! Isn't that Bonaccueil?" asked Carmen, surprised. "Where have you been? Isn't it a long time since you've come this way!"

"I was in town, yes."

"Were you? And everybody up there, how are they?"

"No worse off, cousin. Is Zinzin here?"

"He went to cut some wood. He won't be long, for night's coming on. Won't you sit down?"

"Thank you. I will."

Bonaccueil was an "habitant," a countryman, a true Negro of the hills. He wore a yellow foulard knotted around his head and the traditional dark-blue blouse. He put his straw knapsack in a corner with his stick and hat, and sat down full of ceremony, with his fists on his knees.

Cupping her hands over her mouth, Carmen called Zinzin. The noise of his machete, whose echo borne on the wind reached the house, ceased at once. She called him again.

"Hou-hou!" he answered.

"Someone here to see you!"

Night had gradually gained ground. First the shadow, that all day had lain splotched in little puddles at the foot of the trees and in the hollows of the ravines and gorges, grew denser; the darkness, drawing in her fragments, had reunited and fused them into a single mass. Now they arose, reaching in silence the heights of the heavens.

Anacius teased Orphise into playing the nocturnal game of riddles.

"Time—time!" he started off in an impudent voice.

"Bois sec! Dry wood!" Orphise replied softly.

"How many branches?"

"Five branches!"

It was only play but Anacius was angry and promised to beat his sister at the game for having limited him to five riddles.

"Cric!" said he peevishly.

"Crac!"

"I give drink, food, and something to throw away."

"Coconut!"

"Cric!"

"Crac!"

"Water standing up."

"Sugar cane!"

"Cric!"

"Crac!"

"Water lying down."

"A melon!"

"Cric!"

"Crac!"

"Lacatao fait cao. It can be heard as far as Guinea."

"The thunder!"

"Cric!"

"Crac!"

"Here I am, grasp me, if you can!"

"Shadow! . . ."

"How goes it, Bonaccueil?" said Zinzin, coming up.

"So so, yes, cousin. I just dropped by to say good evening on my way to Carrefour-Laboule. And over here, how is everything?"

"Ah! Bonaccueil, things are not very good. They're not at all good."

He rid himself of his bundle of faggots with a quick thrust of his shoulder as if he wished to free himself, at the same time, of all the worries that were crushing him down.

"Like that?" said Bonaccueil, clicking his tongue with astonishment.

"Like that exactly. Didn't you see how red the sky was last night?"

"Yes," replied Bonaccueil, "the sky was so red that one would have thought it was bleeding!"

Zinzin picked up a chair, propped it against one of the supports of the arbor and sank down in it full of weariness and presentments. Then he called to his wife. "Carmen, go buy me ten cents' worth of rum at Sor Mélie's."

"Where's the money?" she asked.

"Get it on account."

"What account, Zinzin? Hasn't Sor Mélie closed it?"

"Ayayaye, woman! What business have you to talk like that? You've only got to do what I tell you. The rest is none of your affair. . . ."

Orphise had answered Anacius' conundrums. Now she was the one who questioned.

"Maker of mats sleeps on the ground."

Anacius couldn't answer, but being a dishonest brat he did not want to admit he was stumped.

"That's not a riddle," said he. "Give me another."

"Answer this one first!"

"I won't. It's too easy."

"Answer just the same."

"I don't want to."

"You don't want to," jeered Orphise. "Admit that you don't know, or answer the question. Maker of mats sleeps on the ground."

"Pumpkin!" whispered Bonaccueil.

Anacius was angry. "I'm not going to play any more, and that's all!"

Bonaccueil was convulsed. He liked children and it amused him to tease them. But Zinzin, who was in a black mood that evening, put an end to his light-heartedness.

"How is everybody?"

"They're still there, cousin. It's Judge Tiodor who tries to make us go through the eye of a needle."

"Ho-ho!" exclaimed Zinzin.

"Do you know him?"

"Why, yes, Bonaccueil. I know him."

"Well, here's our story and you tell me if it isn't a misery! One fine day Judge Tiodor got us all together at his house. He told us he had received an order from the government that everybody at Carrefour-Laboule must help him to plant eucalyptus trees, and that we would be given a little bounty for it. Could we say no to him? Then we planted the eucalyptus—we planted them, planted until we were worn out. After that he even made us weed his own fields. But when we talked to him of payment, Judge Tiodor called us liars, dogs, thieves, loafers, and threatened us with prison."

"Ho-ho!" interrupted Zinzin. "What's that you tell me? Are you sure it's true, Bonaccueil?"

"I tell you I know it! The first person he got was Cholo. The week after it was Assezlhomme, Vilbon and Louisina. Yesterday he took poor old Dieujuste, sick as he is. . . ."

Anacius was bored. "Time—time," he suggested to Orphise.

"Didn't you say you wouldn't play with me?"

"Yes, I said that but I was angry. Now I'm not any more."

"Well," replied Orphise, "this time it is I who won't play. That will teach you to be more honest."

"All right," he stormed. "Papa, papa, Orphise won't play with me."

"What's the matter, Orphise?" demanded Zinzin.

"Nothing, papa."

"Well then, go on and play with Anacius."

"Yes, papa," consented the child without the slightest trace of rebellion.

"Time—time," repeated Anacius, triumphant.

But it was Bonaccueil who answered him. "Bois sec! Dry wood!"

Anacius didn't wait to be urged. "How many branches?"

"One branch."

"What, cousin Bonaccueil, only a single branch?"

"Yes, a single branch, but it's a story. . . . Cric!"

"Crac!"

"Well, Bouqui, the old goat, has a fiancée. He says to Malice, 'Malice my dear, you know I have a fiancée,' and Malice asks to meet her, but Bouqui knows that he is an evil-minded person so he doesn't want to introduce him to his fiancée. Then Malice spies on Bouqui and follows him when he goes to call on her. When Bouqui leaves, Malice goes to see the young girl and says, 'How can you take Bouqui for a fiancé? Bouqui is my horse!'"

"Ho-ho!" ejaculated Anacius indignantly. "See how right Bouqui was! Malice isn't worth picking up with a pair of tongs."

"The fiancée doesn't want to believe Malice," continued Bonaccueil, "so he says to her, 'All right. To-morrow you'll see that Bouqui is my horse.' When he finds Bouqui he says to him, 'Uncle, you know I'm being married pretty soon. There'll be a regular blow-

out. A steer will be killed, a pig and two kids. It's
too bad I can't invite you to the wedding.' 'And why
can't you invite me?'

" 'I don't know your fiancée, and I can't invite you
without her.'

" 'That's true. We'll go to see her tomorrow and
I'll introduce you.' "

"Bouqui is so greedy," said Orphise, sincerely disgusted. "It's always by his stomach that he lets himself be caught. Besides that, he's so stupid."

"The next day Malice made believe that he was
sick and unable to walk. Then Bouqui gets down on
all fours and lets him get up on his back. But Bouqui
had only taken a few steps when Malice fell off.
'I see what's the matter,' said he. 'It's a saddle I need.'
'You think so,' said Bouqui. 'Well, then you can saddle me.' Malice puts it on and they start off again,
but Malice fell off once more. This time it was a
bridle that was lacking, so amiable Bouqui permitted
himself to be bridled. Malice continued to play the
same game, so well, that in the end he had boots,
gloves, a whip and spurs."

"Oh, oh, oh!" exclaimed Anacius. "Orphise is
right. Bouqui is surely a fool!"

"Bon! They start out in earnest this time. Bouqui
walks, he trots, he gallops, he sweats. At last they
arrive at the fiancée's house. Malice rakes Bouqui with
his spurs, who enters the yard pawing the ground.

Malice ties him to a tree, and then the fiancée sees that Bouqui is really Malice's horse. . . ."

Carmen brought in the rum and Zinzin, following the rules of peasant politeness, served himself first—a big bumper that he swallowed at one gulp without making a face. Then he passed both the bottle and glass to his cousin. After he had taken his drink Bonaccueil took some tobacco from his knapsack and offered it to Zinzin.

"Among others," said he, "I saw Sanite at midday. Poor devil! If you could see how she has changed! You wouldn't recognize her."

Zinzin made believe he hadn't heard. He distrusted Bonaccueil's tongue. It had made him some enemies in the past. So, to put an end to any indiscretion, he asked, "Haven't I been told, cousin, that you are well on the road to making the race of roosters disappear at Carrefour-Laboule?"

"Me?" said Bonaccueil, laughing. "That's where they fight cocks. I can only sit and look on. The other day, it's true, I won two bets, but they were not real bets, those! One was for only five gourdes and the other for seven. And then, you know, I lost that same money at dice. If you want to talk about bets tell me about yours."

"That's what you think. If I told you that last month I lost three cocks, one after the other, what would you say?"

"What about Bacalou?"

"Don't speak of him, cousin. Everyone's afraid of him. No one will bet against him."

"Is that so? Well, me, in your place, I know what I should do. We'll make Bacalou a coward, and stage a losing bout. It will bring in a lot of money. I'll make a bet with you on my big black cock—you know him —and we'll divide the winnings fifty-fifty. What do you say, cousin?"

Zinzin became enthusiastic. "That's a good idea," said he. "Tell me how we could do it, Bonaccueil!"

Carmen served the men a small plate of millet, and as they ate they worked out their plan. First it would be necessary to put Bacalou on a starvation diet; no pepper nor corn, no ginger massages—nothing but potato peelings; then the night before the fight they would put him through such a course of sprouts that any little chicken that happened along could pull out his feathers and kill him in jig time. Bonaccueil was to come down from Carrefour-Laboule with some of his buddies who would accept all the money offered on his rooster. It sounded like a good scheme for in the cockpit at Divesco they were not known, and they could clean up the bettors and people wouldn't see anything but dust. . . .

"Time—time!" said Anacius.

"Go to bed!" Zinzin commanded gruffly. "Don't you see the grownups are talking?"

That night Bonaccueil did not go on to Carrefour-Laboule. . . .

CHAPTER IX

The day after Aladin
had broken with Sanite she left Canapé-Vert, not
wishing to see the triumph of the girl who had sup-
planted her. She had taken refuge in Port-au-Prince
with a relative, Sarah, who owned a small two-room
shack in Bois-de-Chêne alley. Like the majority of the
women who lived in that sordid part of town, furtively hidden like a shameful ulcer in the bosom of
beautiful surroundings, Sarah was a prostitute. She
was surprised when Sanite told her she intended to
work. In her opinion that was a silly, country idea.
She too, at the beginning of her urban career, had
nursed that naïve intention, but she soon satisfied herself that the only reward of work was fatigue and

exhaustion. "Work was only made for animals," she told poor Sanite, but Sanite wouldn't listen to her. She had come from Canapé-Vert with her pressing irons and intended to make her living as a washer-woman. Thanks to Sarah's help, she found a few customers among the young people of the quarter. Each day she went to wash the clothes at the bottom of the ravine, not to return until nightfall, worn out; her legs and loins aching from bending over. And her troubles did not stop there, for she had to dun her clients, who were poor pay, and after that prepare the only meal of the day before she could stretch out on her cot.

That she wouldn't consent to follow Sarah's example was not because prostitution in itself was repugnant to her; in other days she had, on occasion, practiced it a little, being then a free woman, but she still loved Aladin and it was physically impossible for her to lend herself to other men's pleasures.

One night when Sarah had brought back two clients to her house, one of them seeing Sanite asleep had tried to take advantage of her. Startled, she defended herself; then when he tried to force her, she aroused the neighbors with her screams. Sarah was indignant and took her side, chasing out the two men. This misadventure disgusted her with the alley, and that very night she returned to Canapé-Vert.

Once (it was the previous Saturday), Sarah had taken her to a ball. She sullenly kept to herself in

a corner, refusing all invitations. Late in the evening
a drunken man, annoyed because she would not notice him, had seized her by the throat. A fight followed in the course of which Sanite was almost strangled. In the end, the police had interfered and, after
a judicious and impartial clubbing, had taken everybody to the station-house. Sarah tried vainly to console her for this new trouble. Apart from the emo-
tions of the struggle, however, it only cost her a fine
and some bruises. To Sarah it was a banal episode of
life in the city; but as to Sanite, already succumbing
to discouragement, it made her want to finish once
and for all, with her misery. . . .

"But understand," Sarah said to her, "life is never
easy for us unfortunates. It never will be easy either.
If we suffer, it is because the good Lord wished it so,
and no one on earth can undo what he does up there
in the sky."

"Then why should we fear death," replied Sanite,
"since we can but suffer?"

"Sanite, you're like a child. If all the poor devils
who are arrested said like you! . . . Me, how many
times have they beaten me up? How many times have
they put me in prison?"

"Ah! Sarah, don't talk about things you don't
know. That's not the only thing I have on my chest.
There comes a time when one can't stand any more.
Then isn't it only to death that one can look for
deliverance? For my part, I've had enough. I'm

through with suffering and humiliation. . . . Don't you know I'm accursed?"

"But all poor wretches are accursed. I'm cursed too. . . ."

"All right, Sarah, don't let's talk of it any more. You don't understand me, you never will be able to understand me."

"And what is it that I can't understand? Ain't I a poor wretch like you?"

"Yes, you are one of the unlucky. But I'm telling you, ever since the affair of Tonton Bossa everybody in Canapé-Vert is accursed. I'm accursed. Aladin is accursed. Florina is accursed. . . ."

"You've already said that, but I ask myself what have you got to expect from it?"

"What I've got to expect? And Aladin who deserted me for Florina? And Florina who left him for José? And José who went to live on his father's land? Don't you see how that works together?"

Sarah thought a moment. "Well then, you would like to have Aladin take you back? I know someone who can arrange that affair. It's Préval. You must have heard him spoken of. He's very clever, you know, at that sort of thing."

"And who told you I wanted Aladin to take me back?"

"Hold your tongue," said Sarah, convinced. "Now I understand everything. This very evening I'll see

Préval for you." She dressed herself and in spite of Sanite's protestations went to find the houngan.

Sanite threw herself on her cot weighted down with an immense weariness. She remembered Aladin's words the night he had driven her away: "I'm tired of you, tired, tired! Don't you see that?" How hard his voice had been, how cruel, how full of hate! With what hostility he had looked at her! "Didn't you tell me you were going? The door is open. What are you waiting for?" No, that man would never agree to take her back, and Sarah was silly to think that such a thing was possible. Besides, she didn't want it either; he had humiliated her so deeply that nothing in the world could make her forget. But hadn't Florina betrayed Aladin in her turn? Sanite breathed deeply. A brief gleam of hope began to break in her soul. It was soon extinguished by the cruel memory of Aladin's words: "I'm tired, tired!" . . . She buried her head in the pillow, as if to smother all thought. . . .

Outside night began in the alley, desolate and evil-smelling. Already after having made the narrow passage a latrine, the young women of the quarter, cheeks violet with pink powder and reeking with cheap perfume called "Pompéia," came out of their dens. Darkness, sordid and clammy, spread up from the ravine, and the paling sky turned to green. The chickens, led by an infallible instinct, perched on the trees that had fostered their species from time immemorial. The bats tumbled from their hideouts, grazed the hovels in their zigzag flight, butted against the last rays of the sun, and silently glued themselves to roof or branch, only to fly out again. In the distance a belated song of children, black and poor:

"Frèré Jacques, frèré Jacques,
Dômez-vous, dômez-vous?
Frèré Jacques, frèré Jacques,
Dômez-vous, dômez-vous?
Ding, deng, dong!
Ding, deng, dong!
Kilic-kilic, poissons suivez-moi.
Kilic-kilic, poissons suivez-moi.
Kilic-kilic, poissons suivez-moi.
Kilic-kilic, poissons suivez-moi . . ."

The verses ended in a tumultuous crescendo of sound. Then all was quiet. . . .

Sarah returned, accompanied by Florian, one of their neighbors.

"What do you want?" cried Sanite. "Did I ask you to meddle in my affairs?"

"No," said Sarah, touching her shoulder. "But we are your friends. You can confide in us."

"Leave me alone!" said Sanite, pushing her off.

"That's not true. I don't want Aladin to take me back. I hate him!"

"All right, shut up now. You've said enough foolishness already, and you've done enough. Shut up!"

"I tell you I don't want it. Get out of here. . . ."

"Shut up, Sanite."

"No! Go your way!"

"All right, we'll leave you," said Sarah good-naturedly, "since that's what you want. But it will be all the worse for you." She was in no hurry to leave the room. Sanite, appeased, burst into tears, then Sarah made two steps towards the door. "I'm going. You have no need to cry. I'm going. Don't you see?"

Sanite regarded her vaguely. "Where are you going?"

"Didn't you ask me to get out?"

Florian hastened to interpose, sensing it was the moment for him to speak.

"I've already seen Préval. He's a conscientious man. Besides, I can tell you, he doesn't work for money. It's little he asks for; just enough for the expenses. . . . Which, nevertheless, does not keep him from being just as powerful as Boispirhaut. You'll see, Sanite! He's waiting for us at this very moment. Are you coming?"

Sanite pretended to agree. "But," said she, "where do you expect me to find the money?"

"How much have you got in your trunk?" asked Sarah.

"What I've got in my trunk is very little. Only fifty gourdes, and I put them aside piece by piece, by tightening my belt, so they would not bury me like a beggar when I die."

"But since I tell you Aladin is going to take you back, you haven't any need to think about your burial any more."

"That's true," Sanite answered without any great conviction, and through sheer weakness she followed them to the houngan's. . . .

Préval stood waiting for them before his door. He was younger than Boispirhaut, of medium stature, and of different origin. Outwardly he was a lower-class bourgeois, without anything that particularly announced his profession unless it was that he had sad eyes and a mysterious mien. His father, who used to keep a grocery store at the gate of Saint-Joseph, had taken an interest in his education. He had dreamed of a brilliant career for Préval in law and politics, but a strange malady had overtaken him in the middle of his growth, when he was finishing his fourth year in the Pétion high school, and he was forced to abandon his studies. The doctors who were consulted spoke of nervous disorders, prescribed expensive treatments, but at the end of three years Préval had visions. Night and day he conversed with the spirits. His father, at last, understood and took him to a houngan, who cured his disease in a few months. It was in this way that Préval was converted to Vodun, and he became one of its most fervent adepts. In return the loas visited him often and there was no "service" (or group of Vodun gods) where one at least was not pleased to "possess" him. These repeated favors brought about his initiation into the highest grades of the priesthood. At his father's death, Préval fell heir to the mystères, or family spirits, and the houmfor at Carrefour-Feuilles. This was the history of Préval. It is true he had less prestige than Boispirhaut, whose fame was, by that time, solidly founded as much by merit as by legend, but his young colleague, Préval, was just beginning. . . .

Sanite's impression of him was not of the best. He seemed very insignificant to her, almost a simpleton. After looking him up and down she had an immediate desire to leave, but Préval talked to the point.

"I knew very well that you would come," said he. "Sarah told me everything. I understand what is the matter. It is Baron Samedi that I must call up for you, because it is he who has the entire affair in his hands. But you know how difficult he is. The matter calls for some money and you couldn't have very much."

"How much?" demanded Sanite, with a distrustful and almost hostile air.

"That depends; two or three hundred gourdes."

"And where do you think a poor unfortunate like me could get all that?"

Préval smiled sadly. "It's not I who wants it that way. It's Baron Samedi. But tell me how much you can give and I'll see if there's some other way of doing it . . . with Nibo, perhaps . . . he isn't so exacting . . . fifty gourdes would satisfy him . . . he's a guédé like the Baron, and he could reach an understanding with him in your affair with Aladin."

"That's good," said Sanite, pretending to go away. "I see that you are all plotting together to bleed me."

"What an idea!" protested Préval. "Nibo himself will confirm what I tell you, because I am going to let you see him in person. You'll speak with him. I'll speak with him, too. And he'll tell us what must be done . . . You see I'm not trying to fool you."

"And when will you let me see him?"

"This very night, if you want, at the cemetery on the hill above here."

"No!" said Sanite, impressed. "Not tonight; the day after tomorrow."

"As you wish," answered Préval. "But don't forget the money. It's very important, you know. . . ."

CHAPTER X

Prévilon didn't have a chance. "No! No! No! Isn't this a persecution!" he said to himself. He was returning from Zinzin's where he assisted in preparing for the cockfight, and he was thinking bitterly that he had no money to bet on this sure thing. There wasn't the slightest risk, for the treatment inflicted on Bacalou offered every guaranty. They had soaked his feet in water, half hung him by his beak, and all that afternoon and night he was to be left in that position. "If tomorrow he's able to give even a single spur-stroke, you can cut off my head," Ti-Dan had declared, and he wasn't a child at that game, thank God.

No, truly, Prévilon had no luck. If only Grande

Da was a good old mother who had confidence in her son . . . in a word, a broad-minded person who understood things. On the whole he was a serious man, he, Prévilon! Always filled with such good intentions! She might have helped him get rid of his bad luck, with the assistance of Grande Erzilie, but she wasn't willing to pay for it. Wouldn't it be enough to free him of the mystère who tormented him? But Grande Da never had the slightest consideration for him. Look how she treated him the day of Tonton Bossa's death. Besides, she was avaricious. Nothing in the world would persuade her to touch her savings. . . .

Thus sadly Prévilon reasoned on his way home. To behave badly, according to him, was not to gamble but to lose. A man of good fortune is as respected as a rich man, he thought. Strange as it may seem, Prévilon thirsted to be well thought of. . . . And to say that with only ten gourdes, playing odds of one against five on Bonaccueil's cock, he might win fifty gourdes—a real fortune! With that money he would go straight to Boispirhaut, who would bewitch his hand so he could win any bet he made; Prévilon began to feel vaguely that the whole world was unjust. A blind anger swept over him. He stamped his foot. "That's all right!" he said between his teeth. "One of these days they'll see how much weight I have. I won't say any more." But he didn't have the wildest idea how to bring this about. While waiting for some suggestion he rushed into his house like an angry tiger, pushing everyone aside, took a chair and propped it against a post of the arbor with a brutal gesture. "I don't say any more!" he repeated, sitting down.

"What's the matter, now?" demanded Lamercie.

"You'll know someday!"

Lamercie shrugged her shoulders. She wanted to pretend indifference, but Prévilon knew from experience that her heart held the essence of tenderness and was easily touched, so he changed his tune. "It's not meant for you, what I say." As Lamercie did not reply, he continued, "It's tomorrow, yes, that they're going to have the cockfight."

"Ah! That's so," she said absent-mindedly, "it's tomorrow."

"Yes, it's tomorrow. All those men are going to make money; Zinzin, Ti-Dan, Bobo, Aladin, even those up at Carrefour-Laboule who are coming down with Bonaccueil to make sure of the trick. It's only me who won't make any."

"And why not?"

"Because I haven't any money to bet with."

"And why haven't you got any?"

"Why? Do I know?"

"Well, I know why. It's because you drink and you lose everything you've got at gambling."

"Don't say that, Lamercie. Don't talk like the others! You know very well it's not my fault if I have a jinx. . . . But this time the fight is not a question of chance. It's a sure thing. Everything is all set. I was at Zinzin's a little while ago. Even if the devil himself wanted it Bacalou couldn't make the weakest strike. . . . I must tell you, too, that if I could bet my share like the others, I'd go to see Boispirhaut immediately to have him give luck to my hand."

Lamercie weakened. "How much would you need for that?"

"Not much! Only ten gourdes. If you could only borrow them from Grande Da . . ."

"Are you crazy? All that money! . . . No! As for that. . . ."

"Five!" implored Prévilon.

"No, I won't ask her for anything. I've already got too much out of her just to please you. But I've got two gourdes here, I'll give you."

"And what do you expect me to do with that? It's only enough for a single cast of dice."

"Well, that's all I've got so you'll have to resign yourself to it. After all, I can't squeeze blood out of a stone."

"And who asks you to? I only mentioned borrowing some money from maman. I don't think there's anything in that to make such a fuss about. As to your two gourdes, you can keep them."

"That's good. I will."

"Tell me again that it's the men who have no heart!"

Lamercie sighed, knowing that Prévilon, as he always did on such occasions, would string her out with a whole rosary of complaints and reproaches.

"It isn't for nothing that the proverb says it's when the wind blows you see the backside of the hen," began Prévilon.

Grande Da came in followed by Florina, who carried ears of corn in her raised skirt, that they had just picked in the garden at the bottom of the hill. Prévilon prudently shut up.

"The corn made a good crop this time," said the old woman.

"Yes," he agreed, "it made a good crop. But wasn't it you, maman, who planted it?" Then he added to increase the flattery, for a shrewd idea had come to his mind, "Everybody says you have a planting hand."

Grande Da smiled. "Florina, come show your father how fine those ears are."

A little later Prévilon, who was absorbed in his scheme, said to his wife quietly, "Where are the two gourdes?"

"I thought you did not want them!"

"I said that, that way, because I was angry."

"Ah! You were angry?"

"Yes, I was. . . . Give me that money!"

"What are you going to do with it today?"

"First give it to me. You'll know later."

Lamercie shrugged her shoulders and gave him the money. Then Prévilon, prouder than anyone, went toward Grande Da. "Maman, here are two gourdes that I give you to keep for me."

Grande Da looked at him with surprise. "And where did you get them, my son?"

"Do you forget the rooster I sold last month to Bonaccueil? Well, he owed me two gourdes."

Lamercie watched him, open-mouthed, wondering why he lied that way, but Prévilon was imperturbable. "He gave them to Zinzin the day before yesterday, and he has just given them to me."

"And why, my son, do you want me to keep them for you?"

"I don't want to be tempted to go to Normil's tonight. It's tomorrow that we're going to have the cockfight with Bacalou."

"Han-han!" said Grande Da without enthusiasm, as she put the money in her pocket.

Prévilon was fooled. He had hoped his mother would lock up the two gourdes in the hiding place where she kept her savings, but Grande Da distrusted him, knowing it is always necessary to be on guard against men who are the victims of their vices.

Nevertheless, Prévilon wasn't beaten yet. Contrary to his usual habits, he didn't leave the house the whole afternoon, and when night came he was the first to go to bed. He pretended to fall asleep, immediately. . . .

It wasn't until quite late that Grande Da finally put the money away. To be true, Prévilon behaved badly, but his objective was most honorable: the conquest of respectability. And besides, to him it wasn't a question of stealing. It was simply a loan, and after the profit was realized he intended to return the money to its hiding place. As for the rest, he did not mean to go beyond the sum that he needed.

Thus cleansed by the purity and nobility of his ambitions, Prévilon went peacefully to sleep that night. The next day, on the stroke of twelve, he triumphed over his mother's vigilance and managed to get his hands on her savings. Nor did he fail to take out the two gourdes that Lamercie had had the weakness to lend him the night before, for he wished to risk them at dice in the hope of increasing the amount of his bet. Then he hurried away to the cockpit of Bois-Delmas.

There was already a crowd at Divesco's when Bonaccueil got there with Gros-Sirop, the cock he was matching with Bacalou. He sat down in a good place under the arbor near the pit that served as an arena for the birds condemned by the vices of men to an heroic and bloody destiny. The fans looked him

over with distrust. They didn't know what saint he
served and couldn't judge his cock at its true worth.
Bonaccueil smoked his pipe calmly with a mysterious
air, his foot on the cord that tied Gros-Sirop, when
suddenly three men dressed in blue jeans pushed their
way through the anxious swarming crowd and took
their places beside him. They were the three lads from
Carrefour-Laboule who were to assist him in the
fight. Their arrival did not fail to excite curiosity,
more even than Bonaccueil's attitude had aroused,
and no one tested Gros-Sirop's mettle by provoking
him. It was only when Zinzin came proudly carrying
Bacalou under his arm, that people showed a certain
aggressiveness. "Zinzin," they said, "you're pig-
headed! You won't leave your bird in peace! Someday he'll find his master." And the man who spoke
ostentatiously pointed a finger at Bonaccueil's cock.
The audience broke into laughter, so unlikely seemed
any such happening. Zinzin was content to smile.

On the little tables covered with cloths of white
and red, or white and blue checks, glasses and varicolored bottles glistened in the sun. The gamblers
were busy under the spell of cards and dice. Prévilon, as usual, was among the "devotees" of the
bones. At first his luck was good. Within an hour
he had almost tripled his capital, and if his friends
had happened along then and stopped the game the
entire course of his life would have been changed;

but they didn't. Fate had willed that Zinzin arrive too late. . . . Prévilon lost. . . .

"Zinzin," repeated the same man, "you look worried today about your Bacalou."

Zinzin had pretended to hesitate at the first provocation, but this time he made his way brusquely toward Bonaccueil's cock and held out his own. Bonaccueil quickly picked up Gros-Sirop, glanced appraisingly at Bacalou, who was sounding the war cry of his race, and looking straight into Zinzin's eyes, said "Put up your money!"

Immediately a babel of shouts went up from the crowd. On every side money was offered to Zinzin, who passed in front of the tiers of benches, hat in hand. During this time Bonaccueil, with impressive composure, took his cock on a tour of the place in order to accustom him to the terrain upon which he was to fight.

"Where is Prévilon?" suddenly demanded Bobo, worried about his friend.

"Me, how should I know?" replied Aladin. "He didn't come with us."

Bobo went out in the yard and found Prévilon, dice cup in hand. Gently he touched his shoulder: "Prévilon!"

"Leave me alone!" he grumbled. "Don't you see I'm in a fair way to defend myself?"

And Bobo knew it was useless to insist. . . .

Zinzin had collected three hundred gourdes on his

rounds; he turned them over to the stake-holder who received a like amount from Bonaccueil. Each of them, in order to show his adversary that there was no poison used on his fighting cock, sucked the beak, neck and spurs, and sniffed vigorously under its wings. That formality dispensed with, Ti-Dan brought rum to Zinzin, who spilled a little on the ground, filled his mouth with the rest and sprayed Bacalou's body. Bonaccueil did likewise for Gros-Sirop; then Zinzin passed his bird under his leg, rubbed its head under his armpits, and smoothed his feathers. Bonaccueil imitated him faithfully. At last, the two warriors were placed beak to beak in the pit. . . .

Already, as Prévilon had foreseen, the admirers of Bacalou were offering bets on him at odds of five to one, and the people from Carrefour-Laboule were covering them without scruple.

It was Bacalou who attacked first. He wounded Gros-Sirop slightly in the neck, but he being a promenader scampered away and made a tour of the pit. Bacalou pursued. Sometimes Gros-Sirop slowed his pace, but when Bacalou had almost caught up with him he doubled his speed. At last, thinking that Bacalou was exhausted Bonaccueil's bird stopped and changed to the offensive. Poor Bacalou couldn't understand what was the matter with him; it was only with the greatest difficulty that he was able to stay on his feet. He could hardly defend himself when

Gros-Sirop drove his spur into his side. He made not a sound, being what is called a cock of quality. He stiffened and leaned up against one of the posts of the arbor. The audience, stupefied at the turn the battle was taking, stopped shouting. But Gros-Sirop still showed some distrust; he clucked and made believe to peck. Bacalou was riveted to his post, his head drooping and his wound dripping blood. "Come on, Gros-Sirop!" roared Bonaccueil. "Bleed him like a pullet. See! Gros-Sirop, bleed him!" Feeling slightly remorseful in spite of the allurement of gain, Zinzin sadly chewed the end of Bacalou's cord. In truth, it was a pity to see the old champion's finish, not through his own fault but by his master's treachery. For a little Zinzin would have taken him from the ring, if he had not felt bound by those who had put up their money and who would hope to the very end for an energetic reaction from their favorite. . . .

But suddenly, Gros-Sirop raised his head and advanced courageously toward Bacalou who, in a quick burst of strength, seized him by the skin of his neck, gathered all the vigor he still had, and let fly one of the masterful jabs that always had been his habit. Gros-Sirop, struck in the heart, collapsed, to the great astonishment of the crowd. Then it was as if a whirlwind had been loosed. A terrific clamor shook the thatch of the arbor with its supporting posts. Men indulged in all the eccentricities of African joy; some rolled on the ground, others threw their hats in the air. . . . When they recovered from their frenzied enthusiasm, Bonaccueil and his three friends had already disappeared. . . .

"But, but, but!" stuttered the bewildered referee. One woman peddler insisted she had seen Bonaccueil leaving the arbor; someone had called her just at that moment and she had turned her head for a second only to find in his place a black cat with eyes as green as a leek. She had not been surprised but now when they told her of his disappearance she was sure that he had taken animal form.

"And in which direction did he go?" demanded the crowd.

"This way," said she, pointing to the exit from the yard.

"And the others?"

"What, there were others with him? . . . Well about that, my friends, I know nothing. But as for the man I saw leave the arbor, I ask that the Virgin Altagrace will put out my two eyes if he didn't change into a cat!" Her sincerity left no doubt.

The people decided that Bonaccueil and his friends were in league with the devil, and they didn't think it prudent to pursue them. . . .

Stretched on a deep couch of dead leaves, that slowly rotted in the delicate shade of the logwood trees, José awaited Florina. For a week, Grande Da's watchfulness being more or less tyrannical, she had not been able to go to their usual meeting place, but she had promised that she would be there tonight no matter what happened.

José bent his ear to the least noise. He was not anxious, however, for he knew Florina would keep her word. The rich moist odor of the undergrowth filled him with a gentle melancholy, and the barking of the automobile horns coming from Bourdon hill reminded him, in spite of himself, of his life in Cuba.

For a long while he looked at the sky through the mesh of logwood leaves, then he listened to the wind rise and spread under and above the trees in innumerable cool, whispering currents. Far off wild guinea fowl, overcome with joy, cackled impudently. The light sound of footsteps warned him at last that Florina was near. Soon she appeared with the glittering smile of the Negress, at once naïve and insouciant. Without a word she stretched herself beside him. Immediately he clasped her in his arms and covered her with his large hungry body. "What's got into you today?" asked the young girl. Then she gave a cry of feigned astonishment, and broke into little moans of pleasure.

When they had ceased to embrace, hard reality, censor of forbidden pleasure, seized them without delay. The tragedy of their life captured their benumbed conscience. The burning incantation of their caresses had not the slightest influence on the course of events. The world began again. . . . Alas! . . . And now to complete the irony, the braying of an ass was heard. Up there, on the road to Pétionville the horns continued to bark. José did not long keep silent. His past left a bitter taste in his mouth—a past entirely without joy, kneaded with hard work and unhappiness. Florina lay by his side, her eyes closed on the blind pleasure that still lingered in her mind. But José spoke gently as if to himself. "The inferno of Cuba. . . ."

From their arrival on the island of Cayo-Mambi, the Haitian emigrants were put into miserable, white-washed barracks. They were forbidden to go out at night; and woe be to him who disobeyed the order. He was brought down by revolver shots, or the dogs were put on his trail. But in the day, at five o'clock in the morning, even when it was cold, they were led to the sugar-cane fields and were made to cut as much as possible before nightfall, for the work was paid for by the ton. So much the worse for them if they encountered one of the cursed little red snakes, called asps, whose bite kills in the shake of a lamb's tail; the snakes had been released there to destroy the rats, and they destroyed them well—but they also killed the poor Haitian Negroes. In the eyes of the white folks the snakes were preferable to the mongoose, for the latter attacked the chickens. Men were hired but chickens were bought—that was the whole question.

Nevertheless, all that would have made no difference and life in Cuba would have been supportable, if the cantinas of the company stores had not absorbed, in advance, most of the laborers' money. The owners arranged this so that most of the wages would come back to them. They profited every time, and the desperate Negro toiler could only suffer and sing.

Sometimes there were riots. But they did no good. Mutinies brought in the sugar planters' police, and they fired into the mob. Then came the consul. He loudly took up the defense of those under his jurisdiction, and this too did less than no good. Pretty soon the owners were talking with the consul, and life recommenced as before.

The only compensation for these miseries were the visits on payday of the pretty young white girls to whom one could make love for a dollar. They installed themselves in the open air with their skirts pulled up to their stomachs, and the Negroes formed a queue while the pimps majestically collected the money. Sometimes, when a woman appeared to respond to the caresses of a particularly virile client, the pander brought her back to reality with a brutal slap. . . .

Five years had he known the misery of his life in Cayo-Mambi until the night he was able to escape by swimming with two of his friends in distress. He had wandered from town to town, working at all trades, sometimes satiated with food, then nearly dying of hunger and sleeping under the stars. Once even, acceding to his friends' advice, he had become a pimp, but he couldn't stomach so lazy and filthy a life. . . .

Why did José tell all this to his sweetheart? He himself didn't know, if not because it relieved him of a great weight. Maybe he had concealed in the depth of his subconsciousness a secret desire to soften fate. He spoke as one prays—in a low voice, sad, and more and more bitter. Florina raised up on her elbow, the better to hear him. Now he spoke of his childhood. Those days were like a dream to him, and far far away, so much had he lived and suffered since. The trouble had begun on the night when his father, bewitched by Sor Cicie, had thrown him against the door. He got up, his head broken and bathed in blood, but he walked out straight ahead, to adventure. . . .

The summer night approached stealthily and surprised them all of a sudden. After a brief good-bye, Florina ran along the path home. When she reached it, trembling and out of breath, she peeked through one of the numerous holes in the hedge and saw her grandmother stalking up and down the arbor with her hands crossed behind her back. From time to time she stopped, stamped her foot, and then started off again grumbling, "That little girl, ayayaye!" At last Florina took courage and crossed the entrance to the yard.

"Who's there?" immediately demanded the old woman, straining her eyes.

No answer. But a slight form advanced slowly, tentatively—one step at a time—like a wandering donkey.

"Who is there, I say!"

"It is I, yes, Grande."

Florina stopped a few paces away from the old Negress who snapped at her crossly, "Tell me where you're coming from."

The young girl did not reply.

"Florina, it's you I'm addressing. I want to know if you're the mistress of this house, here?"

Florina still kept silent. She stood with bowed head, in a sullen obstinate pose. Her lower lip trembled in blind irritation.

"You don't want to answer? All right then, you'll go back where you came from," screamed the old woman, exasperated. "I'll have no great person in my house. You hear what I say?" She pointed to the road. "Go back where you were and stay!"

Florina tried with a brusque movement to enter the house to get her belongings, but Grande Da got ahead of her and barred the passage.

"Take care! . . . Take care! . . . No impertinence! . . . You'll leave just as you are! . . . May

God punish me, but I would tear off your dress to send you naked to José!"

When Florina tried to push her aside she picked up a stick and commenced to beat her. Lamercie, who had run out of the house at the noise, threw herself at Grande Da's feet.

"Forgive! I beg you, Grande, forgive her! . . . You know it's not her fault, the little one! . . . It's the curse of the dead Tonton Bossa that has fallen on her! . . ." As Lamercie was clinging to the old woman's legs, Florina went into the house resolutely, made up a bundle of her clothes, and left without even a word of good-bye to her mother.

When she reached her lover's house she collapsed to the ground, abruptly giving way to her grief. She didn't cry but her eyes grew large with terror at the threshold of the new life beginning for her that night—a life that she knew must end in catastrophe.

"I asked you to come to me," José said gently. "Why didn't you listen to me? Tell me, Florina, did they beat you? . . ." He leaned over her, raised her head, and her tears began to flow. For a long time they remained there, looking at each other in silence.

CHAPTER XI

BONACCUEIL and his men had prudently waited for night in the thickets of Delmas' woods. They did not know of the miraculous explanation made of their sudden flight. On the other hand, the people of Canapé-Vert, thinking they had already reached the heights of Carrefour-Laboule with the money from the bettors, were disquieted, but Zinzin guaranteed the honesty of his old friends.

"I'm from up there, me, too," he declared. "I know them all and I can tell you they're not the kind of men to play us a mean trick. While as for my cousin, Bonaccueil, it's true his tongue is too long, but apart from that he's a respectable man, you can believe me."

And everyone had believed him except Prévilon, who had nothing to do with it because he had lost all his money at dice. He was in a black humor and he wanted to take it out on the others. Pessimism was easy for him in the circumstances because he had nothing to hope for. But that wasn't the case with his friends, and they didn't fail to tell him so in no gentle terms.

"Thank you, gentlemen. Thank you!" he replied, very much irritated. "It's always that way; if the brittle mapou tree falls the goats nibble its leaves but if the king of the forest falls, everyone says it's rotten wood. Only me, I don't think you can have any confidence in a man who changes himself into a cat whenever he wants to."

The argument carried weight.

"Prévilon isn't wrong," said Bobo. Ti-Dan and Aladin agreed.

"In the main," added Prévilon, "Zinzin was wrong to put those men in the combination." Then between his teeth, he said, perfidiously, "But a Negro's business is never little, it's his trousers that are short!"

"What do you mean by that?" demanded Zinzin in a dry, menacing tone.

"I threw some water and I didn't wet anybody."

At these words insinuating complicity, Zinzin got good and angry. "Take back what you said, Prévilon, if you don't want me to cut you in two like a pig."

Friends interposed while Ti-Dan remonstrated

with Prévilon. "Does that hurt you as much as it hurts us? No, it doesn't."

Prévilon hung his head sheepishly, and he apologized for he was not, at bottom, malicious. "Zinzin, my dear man, I don't want to hunt for bones in your gombo, but if you take it that way, I'll take back my words so as not to spoil our friendship."

Happily, just at that moment, the people from Carrefour-Laboule came back.

Bonaccueil was sponging his face with his neckerchief. "Zinzin, your Bacalou isn't a cock, no; he's a tiger, an elephant, he's a demon! You can see in what a stew he has just landed us."

"Ah, cousin, keep quiet! Keep quiet, don't speak of it any more."

"If I told you, Zinzin, that I don't know these gentlemen and I managed to pull us out of this bad scrape. . . ."

"Without cutting you short," said Prévilon, "where have you been? We thought you had gone back up there. Me. . . ."

"But, Prévilon, let him talk," scolded Zinzin. "You'll only say more foolishness."

"Ah, cousin," sighed Bonaccueil, "it's only when a Negro is cornered that you find out how much he can do. Ayayaye! gentlemen, when I saw Bacalou seize Gros-Sirop by the skin of his neck and kill him, I said to myself, 'Bonaccueil, my dear, get out of here quick; your affairs are not in good shape. Where will

you find all the money to pay off what you've lost?'
During that time everybody was yelling, jumping in
the air, and nobody was paying any attention to us
. . . So I gathered my friends, said a little prayer,
and that's how we went right under their beards,
with all their money in our pockets."

"Bon! But the cat?" inquired Prévilon.

"What cat?"

"Don't you act smart with me. I'm not a child;
you changed yourself into a cat, and that's how you
escaped."

"Prévilon, my dear, if I'd changed myself into a
cat, I'd have told you. I'm not afraid of you. But this
thing you're telling me, I don't know anything
about."

"Then, Bonaccueil, you mean to say that I lie. Me,
Prévilon? I tell you that you were seen. You can ask
these gentlemen. They saw you when you changed
into a cat and escaped."

Bonaccueil shook his head, clicked his tongue and
smiled; "My friends, I tell you I don't know about
this cat business. You can believe me if you wish.
. . . Unless it was one of these gentlemen. . . . I
was the first to leave. . . . Elivois, you who are so
strong, tell me, was it you? You are so pompous!"

"Me?" protested Elivois, who knew better than
anyone else how the thing had happened, having left
the seat of his pants on the thorny hedge.

"I can see by your face that it's you."

Elivois didn't deny it.

"You can tear out my eyes," swore Bonaccueil, "but I'd say again that it was you!"

Elivois, vain and boastful by nature, began to believe that the tale might be true and that without knowing it himself he had turned into a cat. They complimented him about it and he accepted with feigned modesty. . . .

The dividing of the money gave rise to a painful scene. Prévilon, who got none because he had not contributed anything to the pot, burst into sobs, tore his hat, and rolled on the ground like a crazy man. Aladin was touched in spite of his bitterness against every member of Florina's family.

"Gentlemen," said he, "the way we're doing this doesn't seem entirely fair. Prévilon was a partner. It is true that he didn't risk anything in the betting, but if things had turned out wrong and there had been a fight in which we were forced to defend ourselves wouldn't Prévilon have shared the danger with us? You know that as well as I do. That's why I think we should divide with him."

"As to that, no!" said Zinzin. "If you cut off my hands, I wouldn't agree to it."

"Bon!" said Bonaccueil. "If they had caught me, would Prévilon have helped me pay the bets? Where would he get the money for that? It's impossible to divide with him."

"I don't say to give him an equal share with us.

No. But we could give him enough so he could get rid of the bad spirit that persecutes him."

"And how much is that?" asked Bonaccueil.

"Only fifty gourdes," put in Prévilon.

"No!" Zinzin interrupted. "All we can do for him is to give him the twelve gourdes that he lost at dice. And that's already a lot."

Prévilon redoubled his sobs and extravagant behavior.

"As his case seems to trouble you, Aladin, why don't you give him the fifty gourdes yourself?"

Aladin kept quiet.

"If Prévilon was a serious man I wouldn't disagree with Aladin," said Bobo. "But we know what he will do with that money. He'll gamble and drink it away. And the mystère will prison him all his life."

"If that isn't sad!" concluded Zinzin. "A father of a family with a girl old enough to marry!"

Seeing his cause lost, Prévilon got to his feet and prepared to take life as it was dealt out to him. Without any regard for his dignity, he held out his hand. "Well, my friends, if you've decided, give me the twelve gourdes. I'll be content. . . ."

Carmen brought out the rum and he, like the others, drank and soon forgot his misadventure and humiliation. He was even as noisy and gay as the others. For a long time he had lost all strength of character. He bogged down further and further in poverty, and it was clear now that never, never could he come to the surface again. When Bonaccueil and his men got up to go, Prévilon protested. There was a dance at Démossié's, near Bourdon, and he thought everyone should go to celebrate Bacalou's last exploit. The ones from Bourdon-way agreed with enthusiasm, but Bonaccueil didn't want to go, saying it wasn't prudent, especially that night, because he had noticed some people from Bourdon at Divesco's. So the men from Carrefour-Laboule went home, and the others started off for the dance.

Four lamps hooked on posts dimly lit the arbor at Démossié's where the ball was assuming a Bacchic turn. The atmosphere was heavy with noise, heat, and sweat. Excited by the incessant rhythm of the conical drums, men and women threw themselves against each other, clinched, swayed, separated, and clinched again. Stomachs and buttocks twitched spasmodically. Everything danced, even the shadows and the spectators—old people, children, and pregnant women—who stayed outside on the edges of the crowd. There was a general mingling of sounds, forms, smells which did not blend but kept distinct individualities. And if the drums talked to each other intensely, if the melody of the songs was almost mournful, the words were pungent enough, but their suggestiveness was cleverly veiled. A man would address his mistress:

"Çà qui mandé pou moin, dit m'pas là.
Çà qui mandé pou moin, dit m'pas là.
Çà qui mandé pou moin, dit m'pas là.
Çà qui mandé pou moin,
Dit m'pas là, Lamècie ô,
Dit m'pas là:
Djiole arroyo, mes amis!
Rhéllé dit m'pas là, Lamècie ô:
Djiole arroyo, mes amis!"

With the infinite repetition of the African chant, the singer asked that if anyone inquired for him to shout that he was not there, for gossip was cruel.

But the drums, now competing with those of Canapé-Vert, were beating out the tragic destiny of the black race, fashioned of anguish, humiliation, and revolt. Under Ti-Dan's palm, the spirit of the big drum proclaimed in deep and powerful voice that it was a tribe accursed of the earth and would always be. Whipped by Zinzin's sticks, the small Rada tom-tom expressed impotent rage; while Prévilon's nail fetched sobs of feebleness and resignation from the tambourine.

Aladin was aloof from the party. He remembered that it was a night like this, and under the same arbor, that he had known Sanite. He relived the scene with hallucinated accuracy. All the male dancers surrounded the young woman like dogs in spring. But, provocatively, Sanite had pretended to disdain them. Her breasts leaped like twin kids in her blouse which was worn through by them so that only her chemise remained. Her hips swung vigorously from right to left, rising, falling, rolling. She looked mischievously at Aladin, who had only smiled at her. Sanite came to meet him with undulating rump, her hands laced above her head. He had seized her and, stomach to stomach, they had danced the night long, danced, danced, danced. . . .

> "Colobri, oh! ouaye oh!
> Colobri, oh! ouaye oh!
> Tant pis pou jeunes gens
> Qui pas châché femme pa yo!
> Tant pis pou yo!
> Moin-même, Colobri,
> M'pr'al' châché femme pa m'."

> "Oh, hummingbird!
> So much the worse for the young people
> Who do not seek a woman,
> I, hummingbird,
> Will go find my own."

At last, at break of day, he had dragged her into the near-by bushes. How much water had run over

the dam since then! For five years he had lived with
Sanite; for five years she had served him without
fault; but he had never been able to recapture the
intoxication of that night. Then he had left her for
Florina, and in turn, Florina had left him. Now he
was alone in the world. And he had no one to dance
with as he had danced with Sanite, for she surely
knew how; it had to be admitted, that cursed young
thing. . . .

Everybody was moving but there was no gaiety.
They were serious even though there was a certain
animation.

"Lan grand chimin, m'fouillé trou-moin, oh!
La-plie tombé, m'pas mouillé.
Lan grand chimin, m'fouillé trou-moin, oh!
La-plie tombé, m'pas mouillé.
Toute moune passé, yo tombé rit-m'.
Ce moin-même, Colobri!
La-plie tombé, m'pas mouillé."

Prévilon passed on his tambourine to someone else.
He was thirsty. He went into the yard and drank
three grogs, one after the other. But his conscience
was not easy. "It's not my fault," said he to the
shopkeeper. "There are days like this when I must
drink. And I don't know why. Do you think it is
natural?"

"What?"

"That I drink like this?"

"How should I know? Once that you have the money."

"Even when I haven't the money I am forced to drink just the same."

"And who can do that?"

"They say it's a mystère, an evil spirit that persecutes me."

"Oh-oh!" exclaimed the marchande. "You don't say so!"

"Chalk up another rum for me."

"That will be twenty centimes."

"I know," said Prévilon. "I've got money tonight. . . ."

Everyone was dancing:

> "Badinin, badinin, oh!
> N'apé badinin.
> Babinin, oh! n'apé badinin.
> An-yé! ti-mounes-yo dit
> Yo connain quimbé moune lan coeu'
> Main m'pas gain fami passé femme pa-m'."

> "Flirting, flirting, oh!
> I flirt.
> But the young girls say
> They can capture men through their hearts,
> But I have no other family
> But my wife."

"Bon," said the marchande. "You've had enough to drink."

"I'm not drunk!" protested Prévilon.

"I'll not say you are, but you could not dance."

"That's so," agreed Prévilon, and he left. It was unlucky for him, for he tried to take a girl away from her partner who furiously grabbed him by the throat.

"Help!" shouted Prévilon. "Help, friends, help! They're killing me!" He bellowed without even trying to defend himself. In no time at all he was knocked down. His friends pretended to fly to his assistance, Démossié interposed and took sides for Prévilon's adversary, one of the boys from Bourdon, and intimated that they should get out. They did so against their will for they numbered too few to fight.

As they climbed the hill, on the way to the little cemetery with its close-ranked tombs beside the twisting path, Sanite stopped, overcome by sudden anxiety. "Bon, Préval. . . ."

The houngan started. What was that accursed daughter of a demon going to begin now?

"Bon, Préval, you told me you would let me see Nibo. Where is the horse?"

"Didn't I tell you I would make you see him in person without any horse?"

"Ho-ho!" exclaimed Sanite, astonished. "Without a horse! But such a thing has never been known!"

"Nevertheless, me, I'll show him to you," insisted Préval.

The night was dark and warm. It lent itself to the invocation of infernal mysteries, and Préval was glad of it for it allowed him to achieve the greatest effect from his necromancy. To be sure, he did not distrust the efficacy of the rites he was about to perform in the interest of his client, but he knew from experience that it is necessary to impress men's imagination by miracles, either real or false, if one wants to strengthen their belief; and like his colleagues in all religions he never blamed himself for resorting on occasion to pious frauds. This time it was even more than necessary because Sanite had shown a certain amount of skepticism. It also concerned his future, for the least fumbling would wreck his career. He had therefore taken every precaution and had paid a great deal of attention to setting the stage. . . .

A large black cross stood at the entrance to the cemetery ornamented with rags of mourning that hung like Spanish moss. Préval lighted candles of yellow wax and placed them in little niches on the hillock. At once he commenced an invocation in "langage," that strange abracadabra which came

from Africa, known only to initiates. "Zo ouen ouel
ô, sobadi Sobo kalisso" . . . he intoned. Then a
tumult arose in the neighboring cornfields. This mysterious noise resembled the howling of wild winds,
the stamping of crowds, and the roar of rivers in
spate. Préval and Sanite threw themselves down face
to earth, awaiting what was to come. The uproar increased as it approached the cemetery. The candles
went out, then everything was still. At last they
heard something that came nearer with rattling
bones, knocking together. It was Guédé Nibo, the
grotesque spirit of death and phallic worship. He
climbed up the cross, and placed himself astraddle
its arms, grunting like a pig.

Then, to appease him, Sanite and Préval danced
a devilish ronde in his honor, holding hands, stamping the ground fiercely with their feet, as if to flatten
it, all the while singing in lugubrious and savage
tones the litany of the spirits:

> "Diah, hé! rhellé Diah!
> Papa Guédé!
> Diah, kéké! kéké, Diah!
> Guédé Nibo!"

Verse after verse it called on the gods to appear,
and its only real piece of news was that Papa Guédé
liked to get drunk.

"Why have you disturbed me?" demanded Nibo

with a strong nasal twang. "Don't you know that I am, at present, Minister and that I have hardly time to attend to affairs of state?"

"We know that, yes, papa," said Préval. "But aren't we your children? If misfortune comes to us, isn't it to you that we should appeal for assistance?"

"I have no more family. I am Minister, I tell you. Ministers only concern themselves with affairs of state."

"That's true, papa, that's true. But are we not the same as other children? We have always given you everything you like. See the fine cigars and the bottle of rum we have brought you."

"Ho—ho!" cried Nibo, softened.

"We bring you money, too. It's perhaps not very much; only thirty gourdes! But we haven't any more."

"Thank you, my children, thank you," said Nibo, taking the offerings with alacrity. Then losing no time he swallowed the entire contents of the bottle at a single gulp and lit the cigar.

"Don't get angry about what I told you, my children. It is my fault. I'm so plagued ever since they made me Minister. All day people come to disturb me asking for positions, and when I tell them there aren't any, they ask for money. My entire time is taken up that way. You talk of complications! If it was still as it used to be in the old days when it was possible to make jobs, but you know since the whites have controlled the country's money, no one can pick up even the smallest crumb!"

"That's a nuisance, papa!" groaned Préval.

"And that's nothing, my children. The worst is that I can't write. Turn my pencil as I will all I get is tuzzy-muzzy, oh!"

Bursting with laughter he jumped down from the cross and began a danse du ventre:

> "Plume, oh! plume, oh!
> Cé plume, oh! m'mandé"

> "Tail—oh, oh!
> It's tail—oh! that I want."

Préval joined, clapping his hands rhythmically:

> "Plume, oh! plume, oh!
> Assez mandé plume, oh!"

"Cease demanding tail-oh!" But Nibo was stubborn.

> "Plume, oh! plume, oh!
> Cé plume, oh! m'mandé!"

he repeated. Suddenly he bounded towards the cross, kissed it, and with an enormous wooden phallus fixed between his legs, gave a lusty imitation of the

sexual act. Préval sang on, assisted by Sanite, who
feared lest the Guédé, or spirit might turn his bawdy
fury on her:

"Plume, oh! plume, oh!
Assez mandé plume, oh!"

The hysteria of Nibo was mounting to a crisis:
"This woman isn't any good," said he furiously
as he made a gesture of pushing the cross away.
"She's no more responsive than a piece of wood."
And he threw himself on Sanite, upset her and tried
to raise her skirt. Screaming she defended herself.
Nibo sung with all his might:

"Plume, oh! plume, oh!
Cé plume, oh! m'mandé!"

But in the struggle his voice lost the nasal quality,
characteristic of the guédés and Sanite thought she
recognized the familiar tones of Sarah's friend. As
loud as she could she shouted:
"Help! The robbers are killing me!"
"What do you think you are doing?" asked Préval.
"You'll spoil everything, Sanite."
"Thief!" she replied.
Her dress was torn by her assailant's efforts. She
felt the touch of the phallus on her flesh. Horror
released her strength; she escaped from the man's

clutches, pushing him back on the chin. Then she spit in his face. Préval was indignant.

"What am I doing here? What am I doing? Wait, you'll see. You think I didn't recognize Florian?"

"Florian!" said Préval, confounded.

And Sanite slapped him.

They had trouble getting Prévilon back to Grande Da's. Terribly excited, he talked of returning to Démossié's to show his adversary what kind of man he was, for he said, not without some truth, that if he had been knocked down it was because he had been taken by surprise. On the other hand, it was clear he was as drunk as a monkey and his legs could only just carry him. His friends had to employ a little trick to pacify him. They suggested he take a few more drinks to bolster his courage, knowing he would never refuse such an invitation, so he did not have to be urged to follow them to Zinzin's where he drank until he fell down, full length. Then lifting him by the arms and legs they took him home. Grande Da had received them curtly, even accusing them of having dragged her poor son along the road to perdition.

Thinking of that scene Aladin felt only pity for the man who had almost been his father-in-law. Certainly Prévilon was inclined to drink but he had never been known to be so unreasonable before Florina had let José seduce her. "Poor Prévilon!" said Aladin as sadly as if he were speaking at his grave. And he twisted and turned on his mat, as he had done innumerable times since he had gone to bed that night. Sleep refused to come in spite of the great weariness that he felt. It was because he had revisited the arbor where Florina used to receive him at dusk that a poignant sadness kept his eyes wide open in the darkness.

Suddenly he was startled by a knock on his door. "Who's there?" he called nervously, getting up.

"It's me, yes, Aladin."

He thought he recognized Sanite's voice but he couldn't believe it. The thing was impossible.

"I beg you, Aladin, open the door for me."

It was indeed Sanite, but some demon might have assumed her voice to fool him. If it really was Sanite who had knocked on the door she would have already given her name. At that moment a rat, running across the floor, brushed against his toes. He jumped back, lost his balance and fell down. Fear seized him. "I demand to know who's there?"

"It's me, yes, Aladin. Sanite! Open your door for me."

It was a great relief for him, but he waited a second more to catch his breath. Then he opened the door. Sanite threw herself on the floor and clasped her arms around his legs.

"Aladin, if you knew what I suffer, ever since you sent me away! . . . If you knew! . . . But it would be foolish to tell you, for I could never make you understand!"

He did not know what to say. He was at once touched and annoyed. Touched because he was naturally softhearted, and annoyed because this woman whom he no longer wanted was trying to attach herself to him.

"If you only knew," said distraught Sanite, feeling that her misery was the only excuse for her presence, and hoping to make him repent. And she wasn't mistaken. Without especially thinking what he was doing he put his hand on her head and stroked it mechanically. He was even on the point of raising her up, but Sanite, encouraged by his affectionate reaction, said exactly what she ought not to have said:

"Take me back with you, Aladin. You can treat me like a dog if you want! You can beat me! You can do with me whatever you please! I will always be on my knees before you! I'll lick your feet! I'll be happy if I can only live with you. I'm not like Florina, you know well. . . ."

At the mention of Florina's name Aladin pushed her away, and spoke harshly: "Get out of here! Don't you realize that it's your fault that she left me? You were so glued to me, you made me so many ouanga spells that you brought me bad luck."

"Don't say that, Aladin. You know it isn't true, not true at all. . . . I love you!"

"Get out of here!"

"How you hate me!" She sobbed distractedly. Her last card was played and she realized that she had lost.

"I don't want to see you near my house any more." Aladin slammed his door in her face.

She arose without shame or anger and took the road toward town. Going over Morin bridge, she looked down into the cool, black depths of Bois-de-Chêne ravine. She felt the boundless peace that slumbered there. So she climbed the parapet and let herself drop into it without a sound.

CHAPTER XII

"P ii, pii, pii, pii, pii, pii, pii. . . ." Sor Mélie, the official wife of the chief of the rural police of the district, was feeding her chickens. With a great flapping of wings they pounced hungrily on the grains of corn she threw them. Judge Dor, seated before his front door in his heavy armchair, looked upon the scene with an annoyed, wandering eye. For some time—ever since the day José went to live on his father's land, to be exact—robberies had been committed in his jurisdiction. Public rumor accused a man called Cius who lived at Bourdon; but it never seemed possible to catch him in the act. The chief of police resented it as a personal attack on his prestige and naturally he visited his bitterness on his assistant, Ti-Mouché, whose lack of vigilance he blamed. Entirely engrossed in his worries he paid no attention to his dog. With pointing nose and impatient tail the common hungry-looking cur without breeding seemed to be supplicating in his own language.

"What are you doing there, judge?" Fréquent indicated. "I haven't yet had anything to eat this morning!" From time to time he rubbed against his master who repulsed him with foot and voice:

"Get away, dog!"

And with tail between legs Fréquent returned to sit down in the same place in the same position. Soon he recommenced his annoying maneuvers . . . He lived up to his name, which in Creole means an overly familiar and unmannerly person. What particularly tormented the beast was that Bêbê, the deaf-mute who had served Madan Dorvilus for many years, had just given the sow a mess of potato peelings and bananas, which she was chewing with grunts of satisfaction . . . and he hadn't even had his breakfast. Suddenly Fréquent pricked up his ears and dashed toward the entrance to the yard; Ti-Mouché was coming full tilt. The dog welcomed him with glad barks and capers.

"Good morning, judge," said the assistant, taking off his hat. Then he was silent. It was evident he brought bad news, and did not dare tell his chief.

"Well," said Dorvilus rudely, "have you lost your tongue?"

"Oh no! Thank God, judge. . . . But it's that little pig of Aladin that brings me here, yes. . . ."

"Aladin's little pig?"

"The one he gave Bobo to raise for him . . ."

"Well, what's happened to it? Can't you speak?"

"Bobo got up before daybreak and all he found was the head and feet of the beast. . . ."

Dorvilus jumped to his full height, furious, raising his fist ready to strike, but Ti-Mouché, who was prudence itself, had already put distance between him and his superior.

"Get the hell out of here!" roared Dorvilus, knowing from experience that he could never lay hands on him, so fast on his feet was his assistant. "You think that I don't see you are trying to make me lose my job?"

Ti-Mouché didn't know where to go. He would have given many years of his life to be safely out of his painful and dangerous position, but seeing his sheepish look like that of a whipped cur, Dorvilus shrugged his shoulders with such contempt that he was reassured and, eager to complete his report, dared to finish his story.

"Ti-Dan lost a hoe and two machetes."

That was too much for Dorvilus. He picked up a stick, and Ti-Mouché ran with Fréquent jumping at his heels. A grotesque scene ensued; the assistant waving his hat to the ground, saluting the hothead; at which Bêbê and Sor Tia held their sides.

"I discharge you, han!" cried the chief, unconscious of the ridiculousness of the situation. "And also I advise you never to let me get my hands on you!"

Then as Bêbê was giving free rein to his hilarity, Dorvilus to restore his authority gave him a terrible whack over the head with his stick—a head that was close-shaven, and sounded strangely hollow. The deafmute yelled and ran to hide behind the house, watching awhile to see if his master pursued him.

"As for that accursed Cius," said Judge Dor finally, "he'll know very soon what I've got in store for him. . . ."

Cius had been a famous rapscallion from birth, and perhaps before, even since the time he had jumped in Sor Na's womb. He came into the world on the big road, in the heights of Lalue, one morning when his mother was on her way to town; the labor pains had surprised her at the end of seven months. When, as she screamed with all her might, people arrived to help her, Cius was already out, hanging by his umbilical cord—for she had given birth to him standing up. This was the way the rascal made his sensational entry into life. It was worthy of someone destined to become famous. No one knew who his father was, not even Sor Na, who in those days was young and slept with anyone she met who wanted her.

From the time he had arrived at an age to show character, Cius had displayed a bad streak. Also, at the age of thirteen, he was arrested by the police and confined in the Maison Centrale. There he lived for several years and took advantage of the opportunity to perfect himself in the art of stealing. As they taught him blacksmithing in the House of Correction, he applied himself with a cleverness, which must have been his teacher's pride, but which was equally useful in helping him make a superb kit of burglar's tools. On the very night he was set free, Cius put them to the test. Since then, there was hardly a house at Bourdon, Lalue, or Turgeau, that didn't receive periodical visits from him. Not being one of those specialized thieves who show a marked preference in their stealings, he laid covetous hands on whatever he found in his path that he could carry away, and did not disdain an occasional chicken, turkey, or kid, taken from the peasants. To many his dexterity smelled of the miraculous, and they saw in it the effect of some charm. They even went so far as to insist he could make himself invisible. This, however, was not believed by the authorities. In three months' time, in the district of Bourdon alone, they cashiered two chiefs of rural police—which earned Cius the nickname of "Wildcat."

And, indeed, it could never be said of him that he had taken wooden money or ever been afraid.

But one day, the notary, Volny, got good and

angry. Cius, not content with stealing his briefcase, had the audacity to lift his revolver—a superb, nickel-plated "forty-five," that he always placed under his pillow each night on going to bed. Notary Volny went to see Sor Na, and freed himself of what he had on his mind.

"So, your Cius thinks he's better than everybody?" he said to her in conclusion. "Well, I'm going to tell you something: I come from Cayes, me! You know that's where the most terrible mystères live. I'm going to send a dead man to Cius, so that he will steal without stopping, day and night, until he gets caught!" Maybe Maître Volny was boasting; but ever since that day, Cius' depredations knew neither bridle nor rest. He believed he was no longer responsible for his misdeeds, and many shared his point of view. It even resulted in Sor Na's being pitied.

Judge Dor did not take this view of the matter. Going to see Grande Da, who had sent for him, the chief tried to find out what tortures he could inflict on Cius, when he got him at his mercy, to make him give up his juice like a lemon. He remembered with bitterness that thieves were no longer put in the stocks. Doubtless there were more refined tortures today, as for example the electric current, installed by the white Americans; but, alas, it was beyond his power to employ it, that privilege was reserved for the authorities in town. Luckily he had "Douvent-m' cé-bat' bas," his famous club with its

boastful name, "Before-me-you-must-retreat." "I
pray the Virgin to put out both my eyes, or that I
don't come out alive from this affair, if I don't prove
myself his master!" said he.

"How is it, judge," said Grande Da, "that Bobo's
little boy didn't tell you I expected you early this
morning?"

"Oh yes! my dear friend, he told me; but I was
waiting for Ti-Mouché's report," replied the chief.
Then, knitting his eyebrows, he added, "You know
I dismissed him. He's no good, my friend, no good
at all."

"Is that so?" said Grande Da, and, far from being
interested in the story of Ti-Mouché, she hurriedly
announced to Dorvilus that Florina had left the night
before with all her belongings to join José.

"What else can you expect, my friend?" said the
chief of police with a certain maliciousness. "I advised you strongly to sell the land of the late Tonton
Bossa. You didn't listen to me."

"But, judge, you know it's not my fault: José
is on the ground."

"My dear friend, I've already explained it to you,
José cannot oppose the sale. He can't do it. Trust
the matter to me, and see if I don't arrange everything for you . . ."

Before leaving he asked news of Lamercie and Prévilon.

"Lamercie isn't badly off, no, judge, even though she has had sorrow. She's gone to get water from the spring, because that little pest isn't here any longer to do it. But it's Prévilon, poor devil, who's giving us trouble. Ever since last night, he's been out of his head: it's the wicked mystère that still controls him. You can't imagine what a tribulation it is, judge!"

"Wouldn't it be better that I take Grand-Orient?" said the chief of the district, remembering he had confided his best fighting cock to Prévilon's care. I've got to condition him for next Saturday."

It was an old, one-eyed champion, who crowed the hours with the accuracy of a watch. His neck and legs, bare of feathers and tanned with pepper and ginger, were seamed by heroic scars. Dorvilus put him under his arm affectionately and took leave of Grande Da.

That day,—it was a beautiful morning, like one which follows a rain, with a sky intensely blue and fresh looking,—Aladin was cutting grass for the horse of the priest, who held services in the chapel at Saint-Louis. The night's dew had been abundant and the young man's sickle easily mowed the moist blades, that fell with a gentle rustle. A tart, fresh smell rose from the earth, alternating with waves of woodsy odors brought by the wind.

"How goes it?" said Dorvilus.

"Oh! good morning, judge," replied Aladin, turning around. "I didn't see you come."

Dorvilus put his cock on the ground, placed his foot on the end of the cord tied to its leg, and then, filling his pipe, asked:

"Did you have a light corn crop in August?"

"Yes, judge, but we had a very early rain this year."

Then they talked of the last harvest, which hadn't been so bad, of the low prices, and of the misdemeanors of Cius—but Dorvilus slid quickly away from this subject, because of the disappearance of Aladin's pig. And, perfidiously, he brought the conversation around to José and Florina, trying to sharpen the young man's resentment. He had been playing this game for quite a while, trying to work on Aladin's feelings, as they say.

"When I was young," he assured him, "a woman couldn't have been taken away from me like that. I wouldn't have allowed that from even the President of the country himself."

"But what do you want me to do, judge?" said Aladin, with a gesture of impotence. "If life is like that, then what?"

"Can a person ever know, my son?" said Dorvilus enigmatically. "A day goes, another comes. . . . Can one ever know what one will do?"

He picked up his cock, excused himself, and left, smiling in his beard.

When he arrived at Sor Mélie's, he found the door half closed. He listened, and a splashing of water informed him that the storekeeper was taking her bath. It was an excellent opportunity. He tied his rooster to one of the supports of the arbor and entered the house on tiptoe. Sor Mélie was stark naked and without defense . . .

Dorvilus, his exploit accomplished, stretched himself out lazily on the bed.

"Oh, judge," asked Sor Mélie from outside, "won't you taste a little of this fricassee of salt herring?"

"Yes, please, my little cat," answered he, between yawns.

"It's all ready," said Sor Mélie. "If you want I'll bring it to you in bed."

Dorvilus didn't reply. He had just jumped up, thinking of Grand-Orient that, in his hurry, he had left at the mercy of Cius. Quickly he adjusted the belt of his trousers, which he had kept on as well as his shoes, slipped into his tunic, and went out.

"My cock!" he shouted immediately, very excited, for the animal had disappeared.

"Your cock?" queried Sor Mélie.

"I tied it under the arbor!" groaned the chief.

After his first astonishment, Dorvilus flew into a violent rage, that expended itself in a flood of curses and threats, and bellowed at the top of his lungs.

Sor Mélie chattered her loudest. Soon people came running from every direction, milling around, shouting, so that from a distance it sounded like the tumult of a cockpit. But didn't it also concern a fighting cock? Thereupon, one of the people from the hills, who was coming down to town, announced he had just met a man, naked to the waist, who was cutting it through the bushes toward Jecrois. That man, he insisted, had a cock under his arm. He must be the thief in question, especially since he gave every appearance of flight, and hid behind trees whenever he saw passers-by. Everyone immediately started in pursuit of the robber, armed with machetes, clubs, or broad-bladed sickles.

Zinzin was the first to catch sight of Cius—for it was really he who was the thief.

"Here he is!" trumpeted Zinzin, pointing with his hand in the direction of a tuft of guinea grass. "That's where he's hiding: I just saw his head."

Already the bravest were dashing to the attack.

"Wait!" commanded Dorvilus, and the men stopped. "You, Zinzin, go this way! Three men circle around the other side. Bon! Two men stay in the middle of the road. And five others chase him. . . ."

Seeing that he was discovered and tracked down, Cius quickly pulled off his trousers, so that he would afford less hold, and plunged once more into the grass. A moment later, Dorvilus, who was following events from the top of a rocky hillock, saw him, hugging the ground, slide by one of his men.

"But, hell's bells! Thunder and lightning! Where are your eyes?" he shouted at the man. "Don't you see the nigger's right near you?"

The man hurried in the direction indicated, at the risk of a knife-stab in his stomach. But, naturally, Cius wasn't there any more. In the meanwhile reinforcements arrived. Realizing he couldn't save himself by a ruse, Cius decided to escape by charging the enemy unexpectedly. He cheated the vigilance of those who were beating the grass and the bushes, succeeded in reaching the path quietly; then, suddenly jumping out on those barring the way, he upset them and fled full tilt, in the hope of making the ravine, and escaping toward town.

"Stop him!" yelled Dorvilus' men. "Stop thief! . . . Stop! . . ."

But Cius, finding no one on the road, was gaining visibly. Already he was getting out of sight, and would have escaped his pursuers entirely but, by bad luck, he tripped over a stone, hidden in a tuft of grass, and fell on the ground. Then, from his height, Dorvilus ordered:

"Hurry, friends! Hurry up! Don't you see he's fallen down?"

Cius tried in vain to get up: he had broken his leg. But so obsessive was his desire to escape, that, smothering his groans, he managed to drag himself behind a screen of thorny acacias. There he fainted. When they found him he still had the rooster in his hand! But the cock was dead; Cius had strangled it. . . .

CHAPTER XIII

SHAKEN by a great wind, the house creaked lugubriously. Prévilon awakened with a start. He rubbed his eyes so he could see better in the feeble light of the passing day. His head was heavy, his chest on fire, his throat scorched. His ears buzzed horribly as if all the cicadas in the world had come together; an unspeakable anguish tore at his entrails, and his bowels reverberated with noisy rumblings. A thick slaver oozed from his mouth, and his trousers were defiled with urine and defecation; but he was still thirsty. He looked over and under his mat for his bottle of liquor, but it had disappeared. He suspected some trick of his mother or his wife and grew irritated for, thought he with a mas-

culine slant, he wasn't a child and wouldn't permit
them to lay down the law for him. Calling to them
in a clammy voice, seasoned with curses and ob-
scenities, he received no answer and realized he was
alone in the house so he could go to Sor Mélie's and
drink as he liked. He arose painfully. A sudden dizzi-
ness made him lose his balance, and he leaned his
head against the wall of the house. He rubbed his
eyes again; then when he had recovered from his
lightheadedness he staggered out.

The wind whipped the trees, tearing off handfuls
of leaves and scattering them like confetti; bolts of
lightning tore the dark tents of clouds and thunder
rumbled down from heaven with the noise of loads of
falling stones; the mingled plaints of beasts and
plants, stirred by terror, also were heard.

Having to fight against drunkenness and torment,
Prévilon didn't have the strength to get very far.
He sat down mechanically at the foot of an old
mombin tree on a root eroded from the hillside. And
without delay stretched himself on the ground, over-
powered by the obscure forces of sleep and death.

When the mystères wish to strike they always do
so as if by accident. Why had they waked him just
at that time? Why had his bottle disappeared that
day forcing him to go out to assuage his thirst? And
why had he stretched out under this tree rather than
some other? There was truly no reason unless it was

the will of Baron Samedi. Everyone had to acknowledge that in the light of what followed. . . .

The accident occurred in the presence of Lamercie and Grande Da, who were hurrying on their way home. Bent under the multiple assaults of the wind, which seemed to focus especially on it, the mombin tree groaned to its very roots, resisted a few seconds more, then quickly crashed to the ground. The women, weeping, rushed to Prévilon who was weltering in his blood, his head and chest crushed under the trunk of the tree. In vain they tried to free him, pulling with all their strength, slipping, falling, getting up, pulling anew, pulling, pulling, pulling. . . .

The driving rain would have overtaken them in their frantic struggles if some friends, returning from market in Pétionville, had not come just then. But they were a band of drunks given to palaver and incapable of finding any practical solution. They all talked at once, making the most ridiculous suggestions, without any desire to listen. It was which one could utter the wildest foolishness! . . .

Discouraged, Grande Da sat down on a stone. Two big tears wet her wrinkled, impassive face. Lamercie was yelling for dear life. Luckily Ti-Dan came up in the meanwhile and spoke harshly to the sots, took the whole matter in his own hands, placed the men who were to raise the tree and those who were to take out Prévilon's body, with all the decision of a leader born to command. Then when everyone was

set to go, he gave the signal and inspired them to the
very end, encouraging them to feats of strength with
his persuasive voice:

"Forward! . . . Forward, gentlemen! . . . Forward! . . ."

At last Prévilon was freed! Lamercie threw herself
on him, felt him; he still breathed. A sudden joy
overcame the poor wild woman. She sprang to her
feet and jumped up and down like a merry child.
"He isn't dead, my friends! . . . He isn't dead! . . ."

The rain swept down from the heights of Boutil-
lier and Fourmi. The night thickened at its approach,
and already the roaring of Bois-de-Chêne River,
swelled by the downpour, could be heard amid the
sound of stones and branches of trees torn from the
neighboring mountains. The men hurried to carry
the wounded Prévilon to his house. They arrived just
in time; the first drops were coming down as big as
beans. Everybody piled under the arbor. Grande Da
made a wood fire upon which to prepare her remedies
—salted rum, Boules de Mars (a healing preparation
of herbs and drugs), and poultices of acacia leaves.
In no time at all the single room of the cottage
was filled with acrid smoke to which was added the
nauseating smell of plug tobacco.

The violent downpour lasted a short while. It
swept over Canapé-Vert with fury, descending
toward the town and the sea, washed the earth

naked; then suddenly it ceased, leaving the great black silence of death and desolation.

Prévilon had not regained consciousness. His head was cracked open and many ribs were broken, but with the dressings blood no longer ran from his wounds. Notified by Ti-Dan, who had served faithfully in spite of the storm, Dorvilus came with the slackening of the rain. He immediately ordered that the patient be taken to the General Hospital. This instantly aroused Lamercie's cries and a whole concert of growling and murmurs, but Grande Da cut short these protestings.

"Judge Dor has spoken," she said roughly. "Now no one has anything more to say here."

Then the wounded man's friends docilely placed him on a door in lieu of a stretcher, and lighting torches of candlewood, they carried him as far as the police barracks of Turgeau, where the chief of the district telephoned to ask for an ambulance.

Prévilon died in the night, but the hospital did not return his body until two days later after dissecting it by medical students, as was the rule for paupers. Nevertheless, at Grande Da's the wake had been held. Everybody in the entire region had come to give comfort to the family, and they had drunk, eaten the funeral meats, played, and sung songs just as usual.

It was midday before it was learned that the body
of Prévilon was on the way home. Instantly people
formed a long hedge on either side of the road to
await its passage. They talked with animation and,
as usual, reviewed the life of the defunct. Some ac-
cented his good qualities, others his bad ones; but all
joined in pitying the father who had paid the price
for his daughter's faults, for no one doubted that
Florina had caused the death of Prévilon by going
to live with José—and like a common wench besides!
And this on the accursed land of Tonton Bossa. . . .

When the funeral procession finally appeared at
the turn in the road near Sor Mélie's place, people,
their necks stretching, became silent and their breath
hushed. First walked solemnly Dorvilus and Ti-
Rouge, the new assistant to the chief of police of
the district, then the coffin of white wood carried
on the heads of two professional mourners from the
city. Prévilon's friends followed, singing, to give the
cadence to the march:

"N'homme-là monté sous dos femme-là, roooh!
N'homme-là monté sous dos femme-là, roooh!
Oïdo, oïdo!
Oïdo, oïdo, roooh!
Oïdo, oïdo!
Oïdo, oïdo, roooh!"

The women sprinkled water before the procession,
wishing a safe journey for the dead, giving him mes-

sages for relatives who had passed on, and then
threw themselves in the dust after the carriers had
passed, kissing the imprints of their feet. As the
coffin went by the men fell in behind, joining their
voices to the choir and swelling it:

"Oïdo, oïdo!
Oïdo, oïdo, roooh!
N'homme-là monté sous dos femme-là, roooh!"

It was in this way that Prévilon entered his home
feet first. He was received by the hysterical cries of
his wife and mother.

"I said not to take him to the hospital," sobbed
Lamercie. "I knew they would kill him! The poor
never come out of that place alive!"

But Dorvilus did not excite himself in the least.
"The lizard eats the sugar cane, and the rat dies innocent," said he philosophically, alluding to Florina's impiety. Then he added between his teeth,
"This is nothing! It's only the wedge. The bill will
follow later!"

On the same door of the house that had served as
a stretcher, the coffin was displayed. Grande Da
lighted candles all around it and placed a saucer of
holy water and a leaf of box near the corpse.

The priest came on horseback for the interment.
His cassock, pulled up and knotted around his waist,
displayed blue trousers, shiny and badly starched.

He dismounted briskly, handed the reins to Dorvilus, who, set up by this mark of attention, tied the nag to a tree, stroked its rump, and made an offering of an armful of guinea grass. The women in turn knelt before the priest. Smiling, he permitted them to kiss his hand, pinched the cheeks of the pretty girls, and patted their arms benevolently, on a level with their breasts, but not once did the devil dare to joggle his elbow. He was one of those young Breton ecclesiasts that are manufactured in series at the Seminary of Saint-Jacques, for the evangelization of the Negro masses of Haiti. A fine man in other respects and of a jovial humor. The peasants were pleased by these innocent caresses that he deigned to bestow publicly on their girls. On account of the Sainted Virgin Mary they often brought him presents of fruits, vegetables, eggs, chickens, and turkeys—that quickly went to heaven by passing through his sacred mouth. . . .

The women, dressed in white for the ceremony, stationed themselves around the coffin, and the priest in his surplice began to pray with them. Then came the hymns which the holy man bellowed with the efficient help of the "bush priest"—the old sacristan of the chapel of Saint-Louis, who tacitly served at Canapé-Vert as the hyphen between the church and the houmfor. Then the young Breton sprinkled holy water on the coffin and the assemblage. A simple quick ceremony, and without doubt a trifle perfunc-

tory, but it impressed the warped souls of his audience. Grande Da was so touched that she asked the
priest to come into the house where she offered him
refreshment and a whole string of calabashes—she
wanted to do everything right to secure Prévilon's
soul's safety. As a result of this, pleased by her honest treatment, the man of God followed the procession to the cemetery. . . .

Florina had not attended the funeral, for Grande
Da forbade it. This aggravated her sorrow and added
to her feeling of guilt. Since the death of her father,
she had hardly eaten anything and kept to her pallet,
sometimes crying and tearing her hair, then brood-
ing long hours, prostrated.

José was crushed by this fatality that stuck to him
like clinging mud. To be sure, he hardly knew Prévilon, but wasn't he Florina's father, and wasn't he,
José, the one who had dragged her into the mire
of ill-fortune? Besides, Florina had attacked him
with bitter reproaches that he had swallowed in silence, knowing well that in a great measure he de-
served them. If he had stayed in Cuba as his dead
mother had advised, all this would not have happened!

Then, too, the very night of the accident, a long-
drawn-out cry like a howl had sounded over Canapé-

Vert. He was sure he had not dreamed that! The howl ceased as it reached the ground and burst out again to mount toward the sky. This happened several times, until dawn, smothering the familiar noises of the night.

To José, the strange cry had a sinister meaning. It was a warning from Baron Samedi, to remind him of the debt he had contracted when he settled on his father's lands and to make him realize that Prévilon's misfortune was but a small payment on account.

Since then, hallucinations more or less frequent succeeded each other. So many and so gripping that in the end José lost almost all link with reality. It happened, too, that everything in the house—Florina, the flame of the lamp, the shadows dancing on the wall—took the form, in his demented eyes, of grimacing guédés. . . .

CHAPTER XIV

Prévillon's tragic death
disturbed Aladin as much as José, thus adding to his
personal disappointments an increase of unhappiness
and pessimism. Indeed, ever since Florina had gone
to live with José on the land of Tonton Bossa he
had realized that his misfortunes were only just beginning. He knew from experience that the mystères
(those powerful spirits), fearing perhaps to soil their
hands with crime, only visited their wrath on those
who had offended them through the agency of human beings whom they later condemned to a miserable fate, by way of thanks. And he had a presen-
timent ever since Tonton Bossa's ominous end, that
everything he did contributed inevitably to Baron
Samedi's vengeance.

And was there anything of which Aladin was not suspicious? An Oresteslike peasant, he believed that the curse pursued him everywhere. If he repulsed Sanite that night when pitiable and suppliant she had returned to him, who had led him to act in that way if not the fearsome guédé who, knowing she would kill herself, wanted to keep alive in him for ends most certainly devious the hope that he would get Florina back?

Aladin, harassed by anxiety, asked himself if he still loved Prévilon's daughter, or if on the contrary the sentiment she inspired in him was not one of hate instead? He had such a passion to possess her for himself; to humiliate her! He would have lavished the most expert caresses on her in the beginning so as to make her suffering the more horribly. Yes, he really had that cruel desire within him, but was this all he felt for her? And that irresistible hunger to possess her, to make her cry out with pleasure was a miracle of lust that dominated his sleeplessness. What was that if it was not love? The contradiction tortured him. And Aladin blamed it all on Baron Samedi.

In the end with what could he reproach Florina and José? What was done was not by their own individual will, but by that of the mystères! Finally he came to the conclusion that he distrusted everything, himself included, and even in his slightest act he practiced the greatest circumspection.

One midday as Aladin was sipping his absinthe at Sor Mélie's she said to him, point-blank, looking him right in the eye, "You know Grande Da has put up Tonton Bossa's land for sale?"

"What's that you say, Sor Mélie?"

"Ho-ho! It's Judge Dor himself who told me."

Aladin's heart went cold but he didn't want to believe what he had just been told. "I won't say no, Sor Mélie, but doesn't that land belong to Madan Bossa and her sons? How could Grande Da put it up for sale when Madan Bossa, poor devil, can't speak a word?"

Sor Mélie smiled. "José has his rights in the property, too."

"I forgot José . . . You tell me if Grande Da can sell; isn't it on the farm where José is living?"

"What you say is right, Aladin, but Maître Volny, the notary, has promised to fix everything for Grande Da."

"Ayayaye, Sor Mélie!" said Aladin, shaking his head. "This affair isn't clear, no. Granted the death of the late Prévilon . . ."

Sor Mélie sighed hypocritically, and then asked in her most naïve manner, "How will José manage to live, now he's got a woman on his hands?"

To hide his emotion from her scrutinizing eyes

Aladin pushed his hat over his forehead and scratched his head. "How should I know?"

"Me, I think they will be obliged to give José part of the money for the lands," said Sor Mélie. Then she added maliciously, "In that way he could take Florina to Cuba with him. . . ."

It was what he had expected; José's departure with the young woman! Aladin would lose every chance of getting her back someday.

Taking advantage of his dismay, Sor Mélie asked him, "Tell me, Aladin, since the day Sanite went down to town, did you have news of her? You know I've been told she threw herself into Bois-de-Chêne ravine the other night!"

Aladin's sole response was to shrug his shoulders. "I'm on my way," said he. And he left looking straight ahead, bent under the weight of an insupportable weariness. Mechanically his steps led him to the chief of police of the district.

That day Dorvilus was firing a lime kiln. He had gathered for this purpose a whole gang of poor wretches. It was made up of Negroes of the region who had vegetated in the blackest misery ever since the death of Tonton Bossa. When he was alive they had been able, with his help, to make a living for better or worse, and enough to permit them and their families to dress decently. Now that Dorvilus reigned supreme in Canapé-Vert he wouldn't pay them any more. He even pretended to be doing them

a favor by giving them a few tots of rum and one
or two plates of boiled ground corn for a twenty-
four-hour day of backbreaking labor. Besides he was
the chief, and it was the duty of these miserable
devils to serve the authorities. What were they but
lousy tramps and vagrants who owed it to his pity
that they were not in jail?

Thus Dorvilus reasoned, and the people thought
he was right. They couldn't imagine a different lot
for themselves. Wasn't it also the will of the mystères
that kept them in that state? They were so convinced
of it that when José, following his father's custom,
tried to hire them, they refused point-blank, pre-
ferring Dorvilus' bad treatment to the ill luck that
would be visited upon them if they worked on the
forbidden land. They were the disinherited of fate
and the anger of the loas would have been more
tragic for them than for others.

Sometimes they had the windfall of a little job
for Aladin, Sor Mélie, or Ti-Dan; but what could
they give them in return? Hardly enough to feed
their families stingily. In the days of the late Tonton Bossa, the women were able to help them a little
by also hiring out for hard work; but now they could
only go out at night, having nothing but shreds of
rags to put on their bodies. They passed hopeless
days, as naked as worms, scarcely warmed by the
cinders they powdered on their carcasses, stretched
out on the dusty earth of their hovels where they

lived higgledy-piggledy with their brats in an animal promiscuity. Neither did they complain. . . .
What good would that have done? Doesn't the
proverb say that bad luck is the young brother of
the wretched?

The men busied themselves around the kiln whose
throat sprouted acrid black smoke. Ceaselessly they
threw in faggots. Rotted to the bone by all sorts of
privations, their eyes shone with fever. Their torsos
naked and emaciated glistened with an unhealthy
sweat whose drops resembled pustules, and their legs
coming out of their rolled-up trousers (if the rotten
rags that exposed their buttocks to God's sunshine
could be called trousers)—their knotty legs looked
like frail posts supporting a dilapidated roof, but
one that was too heavy. Thus with scorched lungs,
throats and eyes, they had to feed the fire for three
consecutive days and nights. And the chief of the
district, sitting in the shade of a huge mangrove tree,
not far away, watched them attentively, not per-
mitting the slightest letup, except to eat, to drink,
or to take a half hour's nap. And it was admirable
that they sang to cadence their movements and to
keep up their wavering courage. Some sad songs,
some gentle satires:

"M'pas bouè, m'pas mangé!
M'pas bouè, oh! m'pas mangé!

Cé résignin qui assignin-m', oh!
M'pas bouè, m'pas mangé!"

A sad wail, "I don't eat, I don't drink!"
Even the houngans were ridiculed;

"Trope gangans lan pays-n' là!
Oh! oh! oh!
Oh! oh! oh!
Trope gangans lan pays-n' là!
Min gnou gangan vôlô sirop!"

"There are too many sorcerers in our land,
Here's one that stole molasses."

As Aladin arrived, the chief, in a flood of curses
and complaints, was abusing one of his workers who
had leaned against a tree, exhausted. The unfortunate
seemed to have great difficulty in staying on his feet.

"Dog! thief! loafer!" bellowed Dorvilus. "When
one can't work, hells! thunder! he should stay at
home sitting down and not come to drink and eat
on others. Besides, get out! I fire you, han!"

And the others, as if they had not noticed anything, went on with their work, singing:

"Arroyo! çà raide, oh!
Contribution!
Cé li qu' ap' prend toute l'agent
Lan pays-à!

N'a mandé lá-charité!
N'a mandé lá-charité!
N'a mandé lá-charité!"

"The state takes all the money
And we must ask for charity."

"Good morning, judge," said Aladin, touching the brim of his felt hat.

"Oh!" ejaculated Dorvilus, surprised. "How are you, Aladin?"

"Not too badly, no, judge. . . . You're having a little firing?"

"As you see," replied Dorvilus. Then, casting a glance of dislike at the workmen: "But you can't do anything with such niggers. They come to you, they eat your food, they drink your rum, and then they don't lift a straw. Look! I have to sit here to watch them, night as well as day."

Aladin looked at those beasts with human faces who gave their last ounce of strength, and although his heart was bitter he could not suppress a smile. "Han! That's the way it is, yes, judge. . . ."

"How can the country get along with people like that?" asked the chief with sincere disgust.

There was a short silence between them; then Aladin, with his most indifferent air and as if it was only a question of keeping the conversation alive, said, "Judge, didn't I hear that Grande Da is going to sell the lands of Tonton Bossa. Is that true?"

Dorvilus eyed him suspiciously. "José and Florina have drawn down a curse on the people of Canapé-Vert. What would you have the old woman do now? Mustn't she sell the land to square accounts with Baron Samedi? Because, Aladin, if that isn't done nothing good can ever come for anybody here."

Aladin thought an instant. "Judge, do you think anyone would buy that ground?"

"Isn't that ground like any other piece of ground, if only Baron Samedi is reckoned with? . . . I'm not lying to you, I don't yet know that I won't buy it myself. . . ."

That was all that Aladin wanted to hear. He didn't ask for any more and took leave of the chief immediately. Dorvilus followed him with his eyes, smiling silently to himself, with his teeth bare. . . .

Meanwhile the workmen were singing:

"Çà çà yé çà, Papa Piè, çà çà yé çà!
Çà çà yé çà, Papa Piè, çà çà yé çà!
Papa Piè, m'pas mangé gombo,
Min yo voyé-m' al' lavé assiettes!
Papa Piè, m'pas mangé gombo,
Min yo voyé-m' al' lavé assiettes!"

"Papa Pierre, you see I haven't even tasted the gombo,
But I am sent to wash the plates."

"That's of no account," the chief of the district had said of Prévilon's death. "That's the wedge, the bill will come later." He knew what he was talking about. It was not for nothing that he was prejudicing Aladin. . . .

For a moment, wallowing in complete discouragement, the boy lay on his matting. His face, covered with sweat, grimaced like a war mask. His eyes had lost all human expression. Softly, sadly, without being entirely conscious of what he was doing, he sang:

> "Général Anglessou, ô Bassin-Sang!
> Général Anglessou, ô Bassin-Sang!
> Quand moin songé mounes-là-yo,
> Cœu' moin fait moin mal!"

He was invoking the Vodun god Anglessou, calling him a bucket of blood, and telling him that when he thought of those people it broke his heart. He cried copiously; cried and sobbed like a little child.

> "Général Anglessou, ô Bassin-Sang!
> Général Anglessou, ô Bassin-Sang!
> Quand moin songé mounes-là-yo,
> M' senti m'vlé mouri!"

"General Anglessou, o bucket of blood!
When I think of those people
I want to die."

Little by little his voice rose, became hard and horrible, to swell at last into a roar:

"M' mandé-ou couteau,
M' mandé-ou djara,
M' mandé-ou terrine-là,
Pou m' fini ac yo!"

"Give me a knife,
Give me a djara,
Give me a pan,
So I may finish with them!"

Then, suddenly, bounding like a wild animal, he shouted, "M' hou-ou! . . . M' hou-ou! . . . I want blood! . . . M' hou-ou! . . . I say I want blood! . . ." Capering like a horse—for Anglessou was the rider—he circled the room, breaking everything in his way. A glass was on the table, he grabbed it up, bit into it with his teeth and swallowed it voraciously, as if it were the most delicious food. His mouth wasn't bleeding . . . At last he went out on the road, capering and kicking and pawing the ground. He went down toward Sor Mélie's store, roaring like a hungry tiger, "M' hou-ou! . . . M' hou-ou! . . . I want blood! . . . I said I want blood! . . ."

At sight of him people ran away like poisoned rats; women hurried their children into the house uttering cries of fear. Dogs howled, their tails between their legs! The chickens gave the alarm as at the sight of a hawk. Sor Mélie ran to throw water at the entrance to her yard.

"No," she shouted, "I don't let things like that come here! . . . No! You can't come! . . ." She recited absurd, unintelligible prayers, but all the more efficacious for that, and the mystère that possessed the person of Aladin stopped and held out his hands in front as though to push back an invisible obstacle. Realizing the impossibility of breaking the barrage of magic erected by Sor Mélie, he turned back along the road. But on every side he was pushed away. Only one path was open and that led, alas, to the dwelling of the defunct Tonton Bossa. . . .

Florina was sitting before the door, drifting haphazard like a drowning person in that bottomless intoxication of despair into which the death of her father had plunged her. José was eating inside the house. He had hardly any appetite, but he had to live, didn't he, and also to suffer for two? . . . Suddenly a terrible anguish gripped him; his hair stood on end. And at that very instant Florina screamed with fright. Running outside he saw Aladin advancing, his machete in the air, growling like a furious wind, his mouth red with a bloody froth. José flung himself forward to disarm him but before he reached him a violent blow from Aladin's machete at the base of his neck, killed him immediately. Then drunk with the sight of blood, the mystère rushed at Florina, who had fainted. Killing her in turn he set upon her body, splitting open her stomach, striking, digging, chopping with savage frenzy. His work of death concluded, he bent over the young woman and glueing his mouth to her wounds, drank voluptuously of her blood. . . .

Aladin was horrified when he regained consciousness, to find he was not at home, and what was worse, he was lying at the crossing of two paths on the land of dead Tonton Bossa—it made it clear to him that he had been led by some bad angel. "I ask God's pardon!" he groaned. "If only the evil spirits have not made me do evil things!"

He looked at his hands, his clothes, drew his machete from its scabbard. They were stained with blood! He remembered his desire to kill José and Florina, and in his honesty of heart he had always pushed it aside knowing it wasn't a Christian idea, but the suggestion of one of those ancient bloody loas of Africa, relegated to forgetfulness by the softened manners of the good black people of Haiti. It reappeared sometimes to avenge itself with implacable fury for this impious abandonment. The idea terrified him! And as he was convinced he had been the instrument of evil, he ran away, reached the hills

and started for the frontier. He was never again seen
in the country. . . .

It was not until the middle of the next day that
Aladin's absence was noticed. People remembered
that the night before he had been possessed by General
Anglessou, called the "Bucket of Blood," and that
repulsed by everyone he had taken the path leading
to Tonton Bossa's house. A search was begun in that
direction.

At the crossroads where Aladin regained consciousness, the chief of police found his knife. Seeing it was
soiled with blood, he gave a smothered groan.

"I was sure of that! The matter had to finish
badly!" he said to his assistant. Then he hastened to
add, seized with a vague remorse and thinking he
could thus foil it, "I warned the family. I told them
to sell the property. . . . They can't say I didn't
warn them! . . ." But the voice of his conscience
was stronger than his words notwithstanding their
content of magic. It reproached him for the intrigues
he had woven around José and Florina so that he
could acquire Bossa's property that he had always
coveted. He didn't have the courage to go further
along the path; to see the horrible sight that he
imagined in such hallucinating detail: the bodies of
José and Florina! . . . He never doubted that An-

glessou had killed them, abandoned as they were by
the good mystères. Aladin's machete, all red, told him
enough!

He regarded his assistant furtively with an ashamed
eye as if he feared his innermost thoughts could be
read. "Go up there," said he in a low voice, "and see
what has happened."

The dogs of the neighborhood, guided by their
subtle scent, had already gathered. They had prowled
around the house, grazing the fence with a cautious
air, their tails between their legs. . . . Then em-
boldened by the silence they had advanced step by
step, stopping at times to listen for a restraining
voice, but there was none. They approached the cada-
vers! They watched them for a long time; cowards—
ready to flee at the slightest alarm. At last, as nothing
seemed to announce the presence of living men, Fréquent, the boldest and hungriest of the pack, jumped
over the two bodies and the others followed in line.
They began once more in the opposite direction. Then
they crept closer to assure themselves that the coveted
prey no longer breathed! . . .

When Ti-Rouge surprised them, they had their
heads completely buried in the bellies of the corpses.
The lieutenant promptly brought them back to decency and scattered them with blows from his club.
Ti-Rouge was particularly outraged to find Fréquent
in this shameless pack and did not fail to make him
feel it. But the dogs did not go far from the bloody

scene. Squatting in the neighboring bushes they waited a long time, full of hope, as they licked their chops.

CHAPTER XV

ALTHOUGH the arrest of Cius earned Judge Dor great praise from his superiors, Aladin's escape after the double murder that General Anglessou forced him to commit brought down on the chief's head the severest reprimand. Nevertheless, his case was not serious and had he had the time, in days to come, he might have regained the confidence of the authorities by redoubling his zeal. The unfortunate incident, however, made possible the realization of his desire to own Tonton Bossa's property, but a dumb anxiety warned him that it might well be the beginning of his fall, and the sequel justified the furtive twinges of his conscience.

Ever since Dorvilus' assistant had found Fréquent surrendering to the fundamental instinct of his tribe, with his head in Florina's stomach, and had beaten him well, the dog appeared troubled and crestfallen. He sought the darkest corners, cowering with his muzzle between his front paws; then as if in need of movement he'd change his place to lie down in the same way somewhere else. He couldn't be comfortable.

Dorvilus watched him apprehensively and associating the dog's present humor with the odious feast it had indulged in, the judge was inclined to see a relation of cause and effect. What had Fréquent been looking for in that affair? Wasn't he given enough to eat? "If only he doesn't go mad!" sighed Dorvilus. But this was to be feared. Generally it was in this way, if one were to believe the ancients, that dogs contracted that terrible malady. And besides didn't the dead, whom he and his likes had attacked, have to avenge themselves? Thus the police officer reasoned, and by a kind of irony Fréquent, indulging in an abnormal fondness, fawned upon him from time to time. Dorvilus pushed him away with fear, for the sad, glassy eyes of the dog boded nothing good and he couldn't bear their insistent entreaty.

The animal's nervousness increased. He sniffed everything as if he were seeing it for the first time. Often he suffered from hallucinations that more and more convinced his owner that Fréquent was not

"safe and sound" and that the curse of the dead was
upon him. Sometimes he would stand up, attentive,
listening to imaginary noises, and then he would make
a quick bound as if to seize something in his teeth.
His taste became depraved, he licked the furniture,
the doors, and even his own urine. And he bit everything within reach, he gnashed the wood, the straw,
and ate his own excrement. If a pail of water was
set down in the yard he would go close to it, and
seeing his reflection, would throw himself fiercely
upon it with bared, menacing teeth.

Madan Dorvilus, as a well-informed person, said
the proper prayers to appease the angry souls of José
and Florina. Innumerable times she watered the house
with eau-repugnance and burned rubber, incense,
and asafetida. But the performance of these rites of
exorcism had little effect in the circumstances.

"I don't understand how you can let that dog
run around this yard in that wild way," she said to
her man, outdone at last.

"That's so, Sor Tia!" he replied, with small conviction. "That's so!" And he made a sign to Bêbê to
tie the animal to a tree. But if Fréquent evinced an
exaggerated affection for his master, the hair on his
back rose dangerously at the approach of the deaf-
mute and he growled.

"Look!" called Dorvilus, overcome by a sudden
fear. "Let's see if it isn't against me that that thing

has been sent. The dog rubs against me all the time. But when Bêbê wants to go near him, he goes wild!"

"Han!" replied Madan Dorvilus angrily. "As for you, I don't understand you any more. One could say you are becoming gaga. Give me the rope! You'll soon see that the beast will be quiet."

She went into the house, armed herself with a bottle, made libations before Fréquent, meanwhile reciting appropriate prayers, then advanced bravely and tied him up without difficulty. . . .

The dog barked all that night. It was sinister to hear. . . . His voice was raucous and convulsive. It burst forth with fury, stopped in his throat, then raised its key only to die away in a painful howl. These lugubrious notes that feverishly cut the silence of the night twisted the very entrails of Dorvilus. Sor Tia, on her side of the bed, cowered against the chief, not even daring to say a word to him for fear the evil spirits would seize her soul by taking her voice away.

It was like a deliverance for them when dawn came. Judge Dor cautiously opened the door. Fréquent didn't move. His dulled eyes were almost closed. From his partly open muzzle his thick tongue, swollen bluish and soiled with a froth of mud and blood, lolled. He was in a state of complete prostration.

"My friend!" sobbed Dorvilus, much affected by the dog's appearance.

Suddenly the horse began to neigh. Coming out of his stupor, Fréquent made furious bounds, and as the rope held, he turned his anger against himself, biting his paws and his tail. Then he attacked the cord that tied him to the tree. It finally gave way. With lowered tail, stiffened body, and hate-filled eyes, he slowly approached the horse and bit him fiercely in the leg. The pig suffered the same fate! Dorvilus, with stupefied eyes, watched it happen without a word. Sor Tia was sobbing, while Bêbê, who had taken refuge in a tree, trembled like a leaf in the wind.

Now the dog, having reached the road, ran down toward Sor Mélie's store, in exactly the same direction taken by General Anglessou in the body of Aladin and this did not fail to strike the imagination of the people of Canapé-Vert. Not ignorant of what had been happening at the chief's house during the last few days, they hid at the animal's coming. They didn't dare kill it for they believed that madness was a supernatural ill and were content to shout a warning.

"Mad dog! . . . Mad dog! . . . Mad dog! . . ."

Fréquent sped straight ahead with lolling tongue. At Sor Mélie's turn in the road he ran into Orphise, Zinzin's daughter. He upset her, bit her in the face and continued on his course, spreading fear throughout the region.

About ten o'clock he went home, dirty, foundered,

with haggard eyes and a mouth full of foam and débris. He circled the house several times searching for a dark corner to rest in. Finally he dropped under a tree and lay there, nailed to the ground. . . .

In the afternoon Zinzin returned from town where he had taken his child to the hospital to be treated by the doctors, in spite of the advice of his friends who had counseled him to do nothing, and in case of necessity to call in the houngan, Boispirhaut, as the injury belonged in the realm of the mystères and was not a matter of the profane sciences.

The doctors had ordered Orphise to stay in the hospital and then had questioned Zinzin about the dog, asking him whether it had been tied up for observation or killed, and if it had bitten other people or animals. Fearing that matters might go hard for him and his, he avoided giving exact information. He only said that a dog, from where he didn't know, had come to Canapé-Vert, bitten his daughter and escaped through the woods.

He thought he had come off well and congratulated himself on his peasant shrewdness that he considered superior to that of the townspeople. But hardly had he reached home before the dogcatcher's wagon stopped before Sor Mélie's door, where Bobo was putting down some rum while he listened to her

voluble comments. Ti-Macelin, the terror of all dogs
in Port-au-Prince, got down armed with a rope and
followed by two determined-looking helpers.

He was one of the most popular men in the town
although nothing in his appearance distinguished him
from a workman of the poorest class. Like them he
was shabbily dressed and went barefooted, his trousers
rolled up to the knees. He was surly and sober of
speech and paid no attention to anything except the
matter in hand. The dogs knew well enough and
sniffed him afar off. But so great was Ti-Macelin's
ardor that he sometimes pursued them into their masters' yard, in spite of the law.

The people of the town, fascinated by the audacity of one of their fellow citizens, celebrated him
in song:

"Rhallé raye-là,
Cé Ti-Macelin!"

"To catch the mad dog
Ti-Macelin's the man!"

In other days when pigs sometimes adventured
into the streets of the town in quest of kitchen refuse,
there was only disdain for those of his trade who
were called pig-catchers; and as the height of abu-
siveness, if it was a question of jeering the police who
co-operated, they sang with all their might:

"The police are pig-catchers!"

But since then matters had changed, as one could see. . . .

"Where's the mad dog?" demanded Ti-Macelin in an authoritative voice.

"How should I know, me?" Bobo replied to him. "The animal took the direction of the woods."

"Bon! Where is his master?"

"How could I know that? I didn't recognize it. The dog came from where he left, it bit a child, and it went away. That's all I can tell you."

"Bon! Where's the father of the child?"

"The father of the child? He lives over there, quite near. I can show you the way."

Ti-Macelin had no better luck with Zinzin nor with those who had come to his house to assist in the crisis. He became very angry.

"This thing begins to aggravate me. How is it possible, here's a mad dog, it bites a child, I ask information about where the beast is, and no one will tell me. Well, me! I know now what's left for me to do. I'm going to complain to the police who will throw you all in jail, the father of the child as well as the rest. I'll see if you won't talk!"

Zinzin fell on his knees. "You must understand, papa! We can't talk! We can't! There's a curse on that dog. And besides I must tell you . . . you'll understand. . . . It's Baron Samedi that regulates these matters!"

Realizing that threats could accomplish nothing
with these simple people so obstinate in their beliefs
(which he shared in great measure although his ideas
on rabies differed), Ti-Macelin changed his tactics.

"Bon! Where's the chief of police of this section?"
he demanded. "I suppose there's a chief here as everywhere else. You're not going to tell me that you
don't know him, are you?"

He was addressing Zinzin, who hung his head and
said pitifully, "He's sick, the poor man."

Then Ti-Macelin turned to Bobo. "Take me to
him!"

Bobo was eager to escape from any responsibility
for what might follow. After all, he hadn't told anything, and he was taking Ti-Macelin to the chief of
police and not to the dog. This doubtless was a peasant subtlety but the reasoning of the loas proceeded
from exactly the same logic and was no less tortuous.
Besides, neither the gods nor their believers have been
very smitten with Cartesian simplicity.

Judge Dor's house was closed. The dog was under
the tree where he had thrown himself that morning
after his mad round. A general paralysis was putting
an end to his sufferings. Seeing that he was no longer
in any condition to do harm, Ti-Macelin shrugged his
shoulders.

"Is there anyone at home?" he called.

There was no response, but he heard a feeble sobbing coming from the house. "You don't have to be scared," said he. "We've come to help you." At this the door was opened a crack and revealed a man's face, old and agitated.

Ti-Macelin asked him, "Are you chief of police of this district?"

"Yes, I am. What do you want of me?"

"What do I want of you? How have you got the courage to ask me that? You have a mad dog here and instead of tying him up and notifying the authorities of the Health Department, you let him run wild so he can bite people. And besides, where were you all that time? You're hidden in the back of your house. And that's what you call a chief of police! . . ." He stopped for breath. "Tell me, if that dog still had any strength, wouldn't he have destroyed everyone in Canapé-Vert? Because, gentlemen, ayay-aye! as I see it, there are no real men around here." He looked at Bobo, who hung his head in shame.

Ti-Macelin spat the better to show his scorn. "Bon! Tell me now, hasn't the dog bitten anyone else but the child, or animals?"

Nobody replied. He looked around, saw Dorvilus' horse and went over to examine it. "Ho-ho!" he cried immediately. "Ah yes, this horse has been bitten too. See the marks of teeth on his leg!"

Just at that moment one of his men, who had

gone to make an inspection behind the house, came back with the sow. "The dog," he reported, "has eaten all the pig's belly!"

At this Ti-Macelin's blood rushed to his head. He hitched up his trousers as if he meant business.

"Take those animals to the truck," he ordered his assistants.

Then to everyone's stupefaction, Sor Tia rushed from the house in a whirlwind. Running toward Ti-Macelin she screamed in a fury, "So you are more obdurate than the good Lord? Because you're the servant of the townspeople you think you amount to something. . . . But may the Virgin punish me if you leave here with those animals unless you pass over my dead body."

Ti-Macelin stood firm. "Non, non, non!" said he, opening his big eyes grotesquely. "Listen, gentlemen! . . . It seems to me that it's the women who beat the men around here! Well, my dear, I'm going to tell you something. With me, things don't happen that way at all. What are you waiting for, men? Didn't I tell you to take those animals to the truck?"

Sor Tia fulminated. Grabbing a stick of wood she planted herself menacingly before her horse. "Dare to come any closer!" she cried.

Seeing the decided manner of his mistress, Bêbê climbed down from the tree where he had perched since Fréquent's return. The imposing stature of the deaf-mute lessened Ti-Macelin's arrogance. He even tried to be conciliatory.

"Oh, my friends!" he said. "What a fuss about nothing! That's why you're told that to do anyone a good turn is to fight with God. Look here, I came to help and now you want to tear me to pieces!"

"Ah-ah!" said Sor Tia. "Now you're gentle! I thought me that you were more of a man than all the other men on earth."

"But, no, my dear," protested Ti-Macelin. "That isn't the question. What am I asking you? Only that you give up the animals so that they can be taken care of in town and you won't lose them."

Dorvilus knew the dog-catcher was right. And as he trembled for fear he would lose his position he thought the time had come to say a few words and settle the matter.

"Ti-Macelin," he began, coming out of the house, "I am a just man. In this matter, it is you who are to be obeyed. The dog has bitten the animals. You must take them to town where you can cure them for us. You don't have to listen to what the woman says. I am master here."

"Ho-ho!" interrupted Sor Tia. "Ho-ho! Just look at him. He's master here? That's too strong now. Where were you? Weren't you hidden in the house? . . . Speak up, my dear, if you feel you are no longer a man, pass me your trousers. I'll hand you my skirts."

"All this," said Ti-Macelin, irritated, "is foolishness. Me, I've got work waiting to be done in other
places. I haven't any time to waste here. Come, gentlemen, take the animals, han!"

But no sooner had he pushed Sor Tia aside than
she gave him a terrible blow on his shoulder with
her stick of wood. He answered with a kick that
rolled her in the dust. Then Bêbê, leaping like a cat,
seized him by the legs and threw him down. Bobo,
Dorvilus, and Ti-Macelin's two men interfered, but
it was only with the greatest difficulty that they succeeded in making the deaf-mute release his hold. All
the while Sor Tia sobbed, holding her stomach where
she had been kicked. Much affected, Bêbê went to
her assistance and tried to console her. As he had no
words at his disposal, he did the best he could, sat
down near her and in a low tone expressed his sorrow
by the only sound he knew: "Wou! Wou! Wou! . . .
Wou! Wou! . . ."

Ti-Macelin pulled himself together at last. To regain his prestige, which had been badly shaken in
the row, he scowled:

"I said I was taking the animals. I take them! I'd
like to know now who will prevent me from leading
them off!"

CHAPTER XVI

S UMMONED to police headquarters, Dorvilus hadn't tried to make the slightest excuse for his conduct, for he knew he had not sent the dog to the pound, because he suspected that the spirit which haunted the animal would turn against him, and he couldn't with any decency advance such an explanation; the town authorities would never understand these matters. As a result he was dismissed. He expected it anyway. But what annoyed him most was that he had been replaced by Ti-Dan, who in his eyes was only a child of yesterday morning, in spite of his thirty-five years. "A child I've held on my knees!" said he sadly, nodding his head. . . .

That morning, while Ti-Dan was at Sor Mélie's with all his friends, Dorvilus went by. He was going back to his house afoot, like a nobody, after two days of being lectured at headquarters. He was no longer the brisk official of other times, but a poor old man who was already bent over toward the ground. Sor Mélie invited him in; he refused with dignity and went on his way, without a single friendly gesture for the assemblage.

"This life!" said Zinzin. "Who would have thought that Judge Dor would have finished like that? True, they are right in saying that the ground of Haiti is slippery. The higher you rise, the more it hurts when you fall."

"Those prosperous Negroes," said Bobo, "that's always the way they finish! They've got too much ambition. Let's see! You have a little land, you have a wife and, thank God, you have a few animals; good, what more do you want? But no, you have to go to some big Vodun priest, you have to commit some evil acts. And why? So that you can get all the women!"

"Han!" said Sor Mélie, who suspected she was aimed at. "You've always got mean things to say. Don't you think it would be better for you to shut your mouth? What I don't like about Christians is that they're hypocrites. When a man's on top, they're all at his feet; once he has the misfortune to fall, they think they can play in his beard."

An uncomfortable silence followed Sor Mélie's
words. But Ti-Mouché, who never forgave Dorvilus
for having fired him, thought he must return to the
subject:

"This is how Haitian men are: when they're on
top, they think they must crush those beneath them.
They never understand that someday the stick will
change hands. See, now: Dor dismissed me, and here
I am again an official. If I wasn't a steady man, do
you think that Judge Ti-Dan would have taken me
as his aide?"

Everybody hastened to admit it.

"And then, gentlemen," added Bobo, "it must also
be said that Judge Dor did too much. Wasn't it he
and Tonton Bossa who drew down the curse on all
of us?"

"No, gentlemen," said Ti-Dan firmly. "Judge Dor
must not be defamed. He was the boon companion
of my dead father, Altidor."

"Good!" said Sor Mélie.

"When you see a man doing certain things, it is
necessary to know why he does them. Take, for in-
stance, my friend Zinzin; if I discover he is in trouble,
shouldn't I try to help him out?"

"As for that!" said Zinzin with emphasis.

"Tonton Bossa and Dorvilus were friends since the
time of President Salomon, when they were soldiers
together. And here comes a day when misfortune
falls on the Bossa family; Bossa dies; shouldn't Dor-

vilus help the family? Well, then! Gentlemen, believe me, it was because Judge Dor wanted to sell the
accursed land of Tonton Bossa that he, in turn, is
in hot water."

Sor Mélie triumphed.

"Good!" said she, "to show you how truly you have
spoken, Judge Ti-Dan, I'm going to tell you what
happened to Normil, when he helped out one of his
friends. I heard the story from him."

"What Normil?" asked Zinzin.

"The one who has the bar on the heights of Lalue,
where Prévilon used to go to shake dice. . . . His
friend (Anilus was his name) was nailed to his bed
with rheumatism. When he bent his leg, it took two
men to straighten it out for him. One grasped him
by the shoulders and the other by the feet. And there
were cries, my friends, and groans! To see this wrung
Normil's heart—for this Normil I'm speaking of,
gentlemen, was tight-fisted when it came to guarding
his money, but he was also goodhearted. He took
Anilus to a houngan, who merely looked at Anilus and
knew right away what was wrong. He shut Anilus
up in a room. Then he said to Normil, 'You'll sleep
here tonight, I'll have need of you.' Bon! Night fell.
Normil goes to bed. He goes to sleep. A little later
he feels someone shaking him. It's the houngan. And
the houngan said, 'Normil, get up. You brought me
a man to cure. I'm not asking for money, but there's
one thing you must do.' The houngan led Normil

into his houmfor. The wife of the houngan is also
with them. The houngan says, 'I'm going to put out
the lamp, everyone must undress and throw their
clothes on the ground.' The houngan puts out the
light. But Normil isn't a child. He takes off his clothes
and, instead of throwing them down, he keeps them
in his hands. Then the houngan lights the lamp, he
sees that Normil is holding his clothes, he walks
over to Normil and taps him on the shoulders, 'I compliment you, my dear. It's the spirit of a dead man
that has been sent against the friend you brought me.
To cure him I must transfer this spirit to someone
else. As it was you who brought him to me, it was
you who was to pay for him.' And then the houngan
took a black hen and wrung its neck."

"Bon!" asked Zinzin. "How was he going to transfer the spirit to Normil?"

"Well, that's very simple: the clothes of Anilus
were on the ground. If Normil had thrown down his,
as the houngan had ordered, what would have happened was that the spirit would have deserted Anilus'
clothes to enter those of Normil."

"So, there, it was the hen that paid for Anilus?"

"Exactly," said Sor Mélie. "Now, my friends, you
see what almost happened to Normil and, just as Ti-
Dan told you, that is what happened to Judge
Dor. . . ."

Like the stalks of corn after the heavy rain of the
tropical summer, the figure of Dorvilus, of which
he had been so proud in other days, sagged under the
weight of sorrow. His legs bent, weak and uncertain.
They were the legs of an old man, and one felt they
would not carry him far. And he, so proud in the
past, so dashing, paid no attention any more to his
clothes. He let his beard and hair grow, and from
morning to night, wandering around his grounds or
sitting under a tree, he talked to himself. Sor Tia had
to take the place in hand. The man's condition gave
her grave worry. At times, when he appeared more
cast down than usual, she would go to Dorvilus, put
an arm around his neck and ask, "Dor, tell me, dear,
what's the matter with you?" He didn't reply, but
only looked at her despairingly with his large sad
eyes.

One day, she had advised him to go to see his old
colleague, Boispirhaut, to arrange his affairs. But,
coming out of his torpor, Dorvilus straightened up
for the last time in his life, his eyes sparkling with
fury and hate:

"You are against me, too, you? Listen, Sor Tia, if
you don't want me to do you an injury, never speak
to me of Boispirhaut. Never again, you understand?"

And almost immediately he sank back into his
despair. No more the old Dorvilus, authoritative and
violent, showed itself to poor Sor Tia; and women
are so made that it makes them suffer greatly. She

passionately regretted the passing of the days when
he beat her, for then he was a man—her man! While
now . . .

Nevertheless, another time, Dorvilus seemed willing to accept his fate and recover his interest in life.
It was on a fine evening at the end of a red Septem-
ber. As Dorvilus was sitting at his front door, he
heard the call of the drums coming from Bourdon
hill. Raising his head with a knowing air, he said to
the woman:

"That's my old friend Dorismé who's having a
service."

"You think so?" asked Sor Tia.

"Why, yes. He talked to me about it at Prévilon's
funeral. It was for today, the last Saturday in Sep-
tember."

"Are you going?"

"Imagine it! I haven't the courage."

"Come! You don't lack courage . . ." said Sor Tia
to stimulate him. "Unless you're no longer the man
I knew."

"As to that!" said Dorvilus without conviction,
and he added getting up, "besides, Sor Tia, I promised to give him a hand with the ceremony. I'm a man
of my word, I'm going!"

When he arrived at Dorismé's, the service was in
full swing. The crowd of guests, spectators, and ped-
dlers was dense. It was only with great trouble that
Dorvilus made his way into the enclosure. But, just

as he went in, he was "possessed" by Agaman, the
famous chameleon loa. He shoved everyone around
roughly as he pushed into the yard, and then climbed
to the top of a great male quénépier tree. He did it
with surprising agility for his age, and even though
it was known that it was not he who accomplished
the feat, but the mystère whose business it was, still
people stood with open mouths and the drums
stopped beating. Then it happened that Agaman,
doubtless annoyed by this unusual and discourteous
silence, abandoned Dorvilus. Thoroughly frightened
at finding himself at such a height, he yelled like a
pig when its throat is cut, waving his feet in thin
air. The tragic part was that he couldn't climb down
and, the limb from which he dangled like a hanged
man was so flexible that no one could go to his assistance.

"But thunder and lightning!" roared Dorismé.
"For the love of God, beat the drums!"

The drummers obeyed. And they sang all the songs
calculated to soften the susceptible Agaman. He
made them pray hard, however, and did not consent
to let Dorvilus come down until after a long quarter
of an hour of supplication; but, in order to show his
anger further, he made him descend head first, and
then left him at once. . . .

Dorvilus never recovered from this experience. He
took to his bed, and a few days later, eaten with remorse for the sins he had committed in the course

of his existence, he began to "talk," as they say.
Realizing the end was near, Sor Tia held her stomach
and yelled with all her strength. The neighbors came
running, Sor Mélie first and Grande Da behind her.
Meanwhile Dorvilus had quieted down somewhat.
His eyes dull and vacant, he sang in a soft quavering
voice that could hardly be heard:

> "Bef marron chaché chimin caille.
> M' mandé çà li gagnin.
> Lan Liogane, toutes mounes malades, oh!

> "Cochon marron chaché chimin caille.
> Moin mandé çà li gagnin.
> Lan Gros-Mone, toutes mounes malade, oh!

> "Cabrite marron chaché chimin caille.
> Moin mandé çà li gagnin.
> Lan Guinin, toutes mounes malade, oh!

> "Moin pas malade, m' apé mouri!"

It was a sad, symbolic little dirge, with a simple
wistful beauty:

> "The wild goat seeks the road home.
> I ask what ails him.
> In the land of Guinea, all are sick.

> I'm not sick, but I am dying!"

Suddenly a light burned in his eyes. He sat up on his pallet and, pointing to the door with his hand, cried:

"Roye! my friends, hold him! Don't let him come in! . . . Actéon, my son, I ask your forgiveness. . . . Hold him, my friends, hold him! . . . It's poison that he's bringing me!"

They flung themselves on Dorvilus to hold him down; but he was so excited they couldn't keep him still until the end of the seizure, when his strength weakened of itself. Sor Tia was howling loud enough to break an eardrum. Sor Mélie, divided in her feelings, because her curiosity was stronger than the regret she felt for her lover, was irritated by the poor woman's cries. They prevented her from hearing what Dorvilus was saying.

"But take the poor thing out!" said she. "Do you want another tragedy in the house? See how frantic she is!"

Ti-Dan took Sor Tia by the arm to lead her out; but she fought him off with the fierce energy of despair. It was on purpose that she wailed so loud, for she did not want them to hear Dorvilus' delirium.

"Let her alone," decided Grande Da crossly. She understood what it was all about.

Soon Dorvilus was seized with another spasm of agitation. Now it was Bossa who came to demand an accounting:

"Yes, it's true, it's true! . . . Don't come in, I

beg you! . . . Since I'm telling you it's true! . . . Yes, I killed Vital! It was I who ate the soul of Exanthus and Philoxène. . . . But I ask your pardon, Bossa. . . . It's so, I tell you. . . . You don't have to come in! . . . Besides, you played me an evil turn too. . . . You promised to arrange matters with Sor Cicie for me, and you took her for yourself! . . ."

Dorvilus fell back on his bed abruptly, and hid his face in the pillow. Then he raised his head, his eyes fixed on the entrance to the house:

"There they are! there they are! . . . Protect me, my friends! . . . Why do you let them get at me? . . . Aye! Prévilon, I ask your pardon. . . . Yes, it's me. . . . Yes, Florina! . . . José! . . . Pardon, my friends! . . . I know what I did to you! . . . You don't need to reproach me! . . . Mercy, I tell you! . . . Roye! here's Fréquent! . . . Roye! . . . Baron! . . ."

He raved for three days and three nights, before he died . . . But no one paid any attention to his admissions, because they believed so firmly that all the evil came from dead Tonton Bossa, who had made the wicked agreement with Baron Samedi and had not kept his promises. Judge Dor, they insisted, shaking their heads knowingly, was nothing more than an instrument of the vengeance of guédé—a vengeance which had, in addition, extended even to him.